June Masters Bacher

Journey to Love

HARVEST HOUSE PUBLISHERS
Eugene, Oregon 97402

JOURNEY TO LOVE

To
My Physician and Friend,
Dr. Marvin Beddoe—
one of
God's Medical Missionaries

CONTENTS

PREFACE

This is a story of Oregon. Surely those reading this story and its three sequels will come to appreciate the bountiful land for more than its splendor—beautiful as it is. Although this book and those to follow are fiction, they have a historical base—one which will give the reader a distinct advantage over those persons who are ignorant of the land's history. Looking at the ordered life in the region today— the quiet farms, the belching factories, and the restless streams of traffic—you will realize the process of transforming a rugged wilderness into contemporary existence.

May each of you, as you read, become aware of the yesterdays which made today possible. Reflect on the time when this lovely land was a fur trader's wilderness under a British flag...a time when mountain men, missionaries, and voyagers made their contributions and then moved on. But, most of all, picture the wagon trains rolling down the passes. See the pioneers and their children breaking the sod, laying out the cities, launching boats on the rivers, and tracing out the new roads. Maybe then you will believe, along with me, that it was God's hand that brought them West.

Let us begin the journey!

L'envoi!

Journey to Love

What is faith unless it is to believe
what you do not see; and the reward
is to see what you believe.

—St. Augustine

1

Unwelcome Suitor

Rachel Buchanan pushed back the silk-fringed velvet drapes of the parlor window, but not enough to be detected from the cobbled walk below. Just a crack showed, through which she hoped to catch sight of another unwelcome suitor.

"You should be very happy in the courtships leading up to a suitable marriage. I have prepared you well to be the mistress of any household," her mother had reminded her in the well-bred Bostonian accent Rachel inherited.

Under Mother's tutelage, Rachel had looked forward to

the exciting time when eligible bachelors came calling. *Perhaps if Mother had lived*, she thought sadly, *her dreams would have materialized*. Now there was only dread and shame.

Her finely-arched brows drew together in apprehension as she allowed the drapes to close only to part them again.

If only her father were less obvious! The small inheritance Mother had left for her education had dwindled. The will had stipulated that the bulk of the legacy was to go to her daughter, the remainder to be used at "Rachel's discretion"—a phrase her father quickly interpreted as his own board and keep. The fact that he, Templeton Buchanan, and Leona Boone Buchanan no longer lived as husband and wife made no difference to him. The man for whom she could feel only contempt, coupled with a certain sense of obligation, reassured her many times by saying, "We shall make do, daughter, until we find a man worthy of your charms!"

Everybody in the little Atlantic village knew of her father's overindulgences in alcohol. So the man "worthy of her charms" must hold a fat purse. Everybody knew that, too, including the suitors Templeton Buchanan paraded before her with alarming regularity.

Crushed by his selfish attitude and in need of the loving warmth her mother had furnished in the otherwise lovelessness of the great house, Rachel had stood her ground on one point only.

"I will not marry a man I cannot respect, Father!" she had said stubbornly. "The practice of matchmaking is over. Try to understand that."

Invariably, her words sent him into a rampage followed by a binge of drinking. Always she was compelled to drag the drunken man from the local pub by way of the back door, since a true lady would never be seen in such a place. But, humiliated as she was, Rachel refused to be swayed by his shameful behavior. Maybe love between a man and woman was the silly myth her father claimed it to be. But at least there could be *respect*.

Hearing footsteps on the walk below, Rachel had no time to open the drapes again. Instead, she glanced quickly into the mirror at her elbow for a quick inspection. *Did the green taffeta look as frayed as it actually was?* The mirror was reassuring as the fitted bodice of the full-skirted Sunday-dress outlined her slender curves. Wispy curls escaped from the long, golden braid encircling her head to cluster along her forehead and rest on the wings of the high cheekbones. Rachel wished the matching freckles across the bridge of her nose could be painted out, the way the artist who offered to do her portrait had promised. She wished, too, that her dress were a little more fashionable. No, she didn't! What difference did it make?

Her hazel eyes snapped with indignation at memories of other candidates brought before her so shamelessly. It was not so much their physical appearances that mortified Rachel—more their haughty arrogance, their cold examination of her and her body as if they were buying a saddle pony.

Rachel jumped when there was a light rap on the door, even though she had expected it.

With a pounding heart, she waited for her father's voice. When it did not come, she called softly, "Yes?"

"Miss Buchanan," a rich, masculine voice said softly. "May I speak with your father please?" His name was lost to her as she opened the door. *Colby, was it? Lord Colby?*

A sudden shyness seized her, replacing the anger she had felt moments before. She had never received a young man alone—never. *Best open the door and get it over with quickly. One day I will find a way to escape such humiliation.*

Trying to retain the becoming dignity her mother had taught her, Rachel opened the door. But the words of dismissal died on her lips. There stood the most handsome man she had seen in all her nineteen years.

The stranger towered above Rachel, although she considered herself tall. He looked so—what was the word for it?—*laundered* and pressed. Even his dark hair looked freshly shampooed. His face was deeply tanned as if he spent a great deal of time outdoors, the white shirt emphasizing the bronze face, making the gray-green eyes look out of place. Almost translucent they were, like deep pools in which she could drown. But it was the strength of his jaw that captured and held Rachel's attention.

"Your father?" he reminded her with a bit of a grin.

"Oh—oh, yes—my father." Her tongue was thick, her poise gone. "I apologize for his not being here to greet you. He knew you were coming—"

The man frowned. Naturally, he would be displeased, being over-persuaded to barter for her hand only to find the rightful owner of the merchandise missing. *Well, their arrangement is no concern of mine!* She supposed, however, that good manners dictated that she ask him to be seated.

"If you would like to wait—"

"It seems I have little choice," he said shrugging out of his jacket. Rachel's hands reached automatically to take the coat, but her eyes were on the broad shoulders, the narrow waist, and the long legs.

Realizing that the gray-green eyes were studying her own in kind, Rachel felt hot blood rush to her face. She stiffened. "Would you like a cup of tea, Lord Colby?" she asked cooly.

Her guest smiled. "Colby Lord," he corrected her. "Tea, yes. By the way, I'm Cole to my friends."

The correction only served to embarrass her further. Rachel hurried from the room, grateful for the excuse. When she returned with the tea service, the visitor said appreciatively, "You are very gracious. I suppose there is a young man—"

Rachel set the teapot down with a bang. "Really, Mr. Lord, we both know why you are here. Must we play this silly game?"

The stranger smiled again. "Ah, you are a young lady of spirit, I see."

His hand touched hers as he spooned sugar into the cup of tea Rachel had poured. To her disgust, she felt another

blush rise to her cheeks and realized that the quick with-
drawal of her hand had been too sudden. *I'm behaving like
some schoolgirl!*

"We both know why you are here." Rachel's voice was
colder than she intended when she repeated the statement.

The smile on Colby Lord's face disappeared. In its place
was a look of perplexity. "I did not know your father confided such matters. And I hope you understand my position. I do not wish to cause you any embarrassment—"

Again he reached across the table, this time deliberately
taking her free hand in his palms. A warm shock ran the
length of her fingers and up her arm to lodge somewhere
near her heart. *Such a casual contact and here I am all but
dropping my teacup. What must he think of me?* Distasteful
as the idea was, she was on display.

In an attempt to hide her confusion, Rachel stood her full
height. That, too, was a mistake. She was now under full
perusal of the gray-green eyes. *What was keeping Father?*

One part of her wanted to send this unwelcome suitor
away as she had sent the others. Another part begged him
to stay. Rachel turned with the intention of excusing herself
again only to catch the heel of her high-button shoes in the
carpet's frayed edge.

Instantly the long legs of her guest brought him to her
side. His arm encircled her waist to steady her. "Are you
all right?"

This could not be happening! Rachel Buchanan, entertain-
ing a suitor for the first time without the presence of her
father, was now held against his chest. And liking the firm,
hard protectiveness of it so much she was unable to move.
Trembling, she let her hazel eyes meet his and there she
read concern.

"I—I'm all right—Mr. Lord—"

"Cole."

"Cole," Rachel whispered in a voice she did not recognize
as her own.

Something magical was happening. The two of them were

caught up in a private universe that neither had visited before. Momentarily, Rachel forgot why or how they had met. All that mattered was this moment of togetherness.

She was unaware that the front door had burst open to admit her father until his enraged bellow filled the room. His voice was a righteous indignation which only she recognized as false. And to make matters worse, her father's voice told her that he had been drinking heavily.

Rachel pulled herself from the shelter of the stranger's arms. As calmly as possible, she said, "Father, this is—"

"Get out!" Her father's finger was pointing at *her*!

2

Discoveries!

Angry and humiliated, Rachel crept from the parlor leaving the two men alone. Too late she realized that she had left her handbag on the sofa. In it was the key to her room. To insure privacy, she always locked the door when leaving the only spot in the house she could call her own, the only place to shut out the noise of her father's boisterous, lusty singing, or his violent temper tantrums—depending upon how the rum affected him. But today it was herself she had locked out. There was no way to reach the dining room either except by way of the parlor. That left no choice but to remain in the hallway until the conversation between her father and Colby Lord was finished.

Making herself as small as possible, she crouched near the hall tree, only to realize that she had hung the caller's coat there. Fortunately, her own cape hung from the other side. And with the Lord's help, she might be able to hide in the cape's shadow without being detected and suspected of eavesdropping. Perish the thought of further embarrassment. *Given the many moods of her father, today's mood was the most puzzling*, she thought perplexedly. *Sending her away?*

Of course, everything about Templeton Buchanan was confusing and contradictory, including why her gently-bred English mother, a direct descendant of Queen Victoria, should have chosen to marry him. She realized her mother did not do the choosing, however. For some reason, known only to her maternal grandparents, they saw the lusty seaman a wise choice of husbands for their daughter. And it would not have occurred to Leona Boone to question the decision. That was only a generation ago.

Things were different now—or should be. Her father's ideas were as outdated as this musty house. One day she would escape both...if only she could manage to do so before her father grew tired of what he called her "stubborn dillydallying" and put her up for auction! The man in the parlor was to have been her last chance, according to her father's ultimatum. And certainly this was the best of the lot.

With a sinking feeling deep inside her, Rachel admitted to herself that—under different circumstances—she could have been...well, attracted to Colby Lord. *Ah, Rachel,* the little flutter of her heart corrected, *you **are** attracted!*

Yes, embarrassing but true, this man had affected her in a way no man before him had been able to do. What had gone wrong? This time it was she who had failed to meet the qualifications. Else why would her father...

The question died inside her. The rising of the voices in the parlor made further thinking impossible.

"—coming here under false pretenses, then making advances at my innocent daughter!" Her father's voice was a bellow of rage.

"If you will listen to reason..." Colby Lord's voice, pitched much lower, rose and fell against Rachel's eardrums. She was able to make out very little of what he said. "The loan, as you know, is overdue...leaving next week...needed for development of the frontier property—"

Templeton Buchanan snorted. "Got nothing to do with mauling my daughter...would've disrobed her if I hadn't come in time to save her honor!"

There was dead silence before Colby Lord spoke. "I would choke you for those dirty words, but I don't care to soil my hands. It mystifies me how you came to have such a daughter. But let us not get sidetracked. The money?"

"I'll send it to you. Now leave this house. I am expecting a guest, a man of considerable means—"

From where she crouched Rachel heard Colby Lord's sharp intake of breath. "I see. Tell me, Buchanan, just how much does a good wife bring in these days?"

Above the roaring in her ears, Rachel heard a shuffle of feet in the parlor, followed by a loud oath from her father. Ordinarily, the danger signals would have sent her feet flying to intervene. Today, she had no will of her own. Her senses were numbed by the snatches of conversation she had overheard. A new kind of shame washed over her. *The man I treated as an unwelcome suitor was no suitor at all!* The young woman tried to remember how she had greeted him...what she had said and done...but all she could recall were the moments in his arms. The arms of a stranger! What a story to share at some local pub!

Did it really matter what happened to the two men in the parlor? What mattered was her escape. Rachel was about to rise from her cramped position when the door swung open and the two men stood silhouetted in the light from the bay windows. She crouched lower, hoping the move was not detected.

Colby Lord looked perfectly at ease and his voice was calm. "I really had not expected you to sacrifice your daughter, but if that's what it takes—" he shrugged. "I only expect my money—with interest. How you raise it is not my concern. I remind you I will be leaving for the Oregon Territory—"

The Oregon Territory! The one place in the world she wanted to see. *Oh, if only . . .*

Colby Lord reached for his coat, a faint smile curving his handsome mouth. Rachel realized then that he saw her. Why, he had known all along she was there!

3

Rachel's Shame

"Rachel! *Rachel!*"

Templeton Buchanan's voice echoed down the long, dark hall carrying with it a very thinly-veiled hint of threat.

"Get yourself here this instant, girl!"

Seeing her father heading toward her room, Rachel rose from her hiding place.

"There is no need to shout, Father. I am right here."

"Listening in, were you now! Just like your mother, leaving a man no peace of mind."

His face red with anger, he strode to where she stood, one muscular arm raised as if to strike her. Then surprisingly, his arm dropped to his side and a look of uncertainty crossed his face.

"How much did you hear? Out with it!"

Rachel found herself calmer than usual during one of her father's tongue lashings.

"Enough to know that you have managed to get yourself indebted to Colby Lord. Why, Father?"

"Mind your mouth, daughter! The Good Book says children are to honor their parents. Questioning me can hardly be called an honor. Now, get yourself prettied for your guest."

"Any man *you* have invited here is not *my* guest. Oh, Father, can't you see what you are doing to me? I am not a prize farm animal. How can you—well, *sell* me?"

Did she imagine it or did his face take on a purple tinge? Rachel had never seen him so angry. She would never forgive herself if she were responsible for a ruptured blood vessel, and it was clear that he was out of control.

His thatch of red hair fell over his forehead, and even the hair on his arms stood out like the quills of a porcupine. Worse yet, he had reverted back to the idioms of his native tongue.

Rachel lifted her hand pleadingly.

"Slow down, Father—please do. You know I understand little Scottish. Try to explain quickly before this—this man—"

"Oliver Gugenhauf!"

Rachel's sigh was born of relief and despair: Relief that her father had a measure of his senses back, despair at the inevitability of his single-mindedness in parading her before another suitor—a German this time, judging by the name. And now with the appearance of today's Shylock, no matter how right or wrong he was, she would become the pound of flesh. Her market price would settle the debt.

"Father," Rachel tried again, her voice desperate now, "you must explain to me—make me understand—before we can deal with your debts. We have very little money, but I could work—become a governess perhaps—"

"Never! No daughter of mine will be a servant while I am alive to provide!"

Rachel bit her lip to hold back a stinging retort.

"Perhaps we could sell the house—buy a little cottage. Oh, I would like that!" she offered hopefully.

Hope was shortlived.

"The house is mortgaged."

Mortgaged . . . mortgaged to Colby Lord!

"You had no right," she whispered. "Mother left the house to me."

"Me, *me*, ME! Do you never think of one other than yourself?" His voice was rising again. "You are a mindless creature like your mother. And, besides," he finished triumphantly, "you never liked the house."

"That is true," Rachel said sadly, remembering her mother's lingering illness and that she herself had been a virtual prisoner because she refused to leave Mother alone.

Even now, there was little to remember but the loneliness and the storms which came with such frequency that in retrospect they merged into one—one which lasted a lifetime. But it was during those stormy nights that Mother taught her about the nearness of Jesus . . .

"Answer me!"

Her father's bellow rivaled that of a male lion.

"I'm sorry," Rachel murmured. "I was thinking."

"Would you want to see your father spend the rest of his old age in some dungeon?"

"You know that is not the practice in America. But how could you risk our losing the only thing we own—even if the title were in your name?"

Templeton Buchanan took a step nearer his daughter and lowered his voice menacingly.

"Aha! The title was not in *your* name either. You were not of age—"

Rachel's cry of dismay stopped whatever he was about to say.

"Not of age? You—you mean this took place two years ago—this loan?"

"Three!"

She shook her head in a vain effort to clear it. All this time and she had not known.

Whatever else he might be, Colby Lord must be a patient man, she caught herself thinking.

"So you can see why it is an absolute necessity that I marry you off well. No self-respecting man's going to let his wife's father rot in a stinking prison. He'd sooner pay off the debts. Why, that's what your own mother prepared you for. She saw your beauty and knew you'd bring a fortune. Want to deny that?"

Rachel shook her head slowly. It wasn't true, but her father was in no mood for reason. Something, however, was happening inside her—something over which she had no control.

"I don't want to meet Oliver Gugenhauf," she said in a small voice.

Unaccustomed to having his daughter defy him, Templeton Buchanan was speechless with surprise. Then, recovering, his eyes narrowed cunningly.

"You will meet him or I will bring charges against the man who attacked you this afternoon. That should bring a handsome sum."

"You wouldn't," Rachel whispered, backing against the wall. "You must be mad—oh, *Father*!" She burst into tears.

Realizing he had the advantage, her father licked his lips and continued in a threatening tone. "We could rip a ruffle from the bodice of that dress, muss your hair up a trifle—make you look *handled*—"

For the first time in her life, Rachel was made to feel ashamed of her womanhood. And her father was the culprit.

Had any girl ever suffered greater humiliation?

4

Daring Refusal

An expression of stunned horror lingered on Rachel's face. *How could Father, her own flesh and blood, stoop so low?* His imbibing, borrowing money he never intended to repay, mortgaging property not legally his own—she could forgive all that. Even his shameful exploitation of her as a saleable item to defray his debts by reason of honoring one's parents. *But to drag her through the courts on false charges of molestation?* This her mind could not accept.

As if in a dream, she heard the sound of carriage wheels

turning into the lane which led to the weathered Buchanan house. The sound of her father's voice, too, was a part of the dream. It carried a command that she ready herself immediately to receive her "admirer." *An admirer? A man she had never met?* Some distant part of Rachel wanted to laugh hysterically. The part closer at hand bade her obey Father's order. She was relieved to find that her legs would respond when her heart lay dead within her. Stiffly, she walked to her room.

With an overpowering sense of depression, Rachel made an effort to smooth the folds of her dress and push her hair in place. Then, with as much dignity as she could muster, she left the sanctity of the bedroom and walked into the parlor. There the young lady stopped, her legs refusing to propel her any closer to receive the caller.

What she gazed upon in astonished horror turned her blood to ice water. Even in her wildest imaginings, there had been no suitor such as this before. Older than her father by at least a decade, his face resembled a shriveled apple. His body was hunched over to reveal a shining bald head, his weight (about half her own, Rachel judged) was supported by the two pearl-handled canes, one in each gnarled hand.

"Here she is, sir! Just what any man would order!" her father boomed, ignoring Rachel completely.

The man's watery eyes focused on Rachel's face then moved downward, lighting with interest as they traveled the length of her body. *I must escape,* she thought wildly. *I'm going to be ill.*

But escape was impossible. Templeton Buchanan, quick to see the man's interest, had hurried to his side. Holding one of the "admirer's" elbows, he motioned with his head for Rachel to join him.

"Shake hands with him, daughter, this being the honorable Mr. Oliver Gugenhauf, late Lord Mayor of a Bavarian hamlet. Come on, girl, speak. Cat got your tongue?"

The old man's laugh was more of a cackle. "Well worth

the price," he said, pumping Rachel's hand with surprising strength. "My carriage is just outside and we—"

"Not so fast, Gugenhauf!" Joviality gone, her father's voice was a growl. "There are papers to draw up—"

When Oliver Gugenhauf frowned slightly, her father continued, "Then there's my daughter to be consulted, of course."

The two men were sizing one another up. Neither seemed aware of her presence. Rachel walked to the window and drew back the drapes, wishing with all her heart that it were Colby Lord talking to her father. Immediately, she regretted such a fateful wish. *Were he here bidding for her hand, she could never respect him. Never!*

Aware that her name was called, Rachel turned. It was obvious that the two men had reached an agreement. Obvious, too, that each thought he had outwitted the other. It was then that the idea which had been pushed down inside her for years surfaced and took full shape. It was as if the Lord said in a loud voice, "I alone am your Master!" And she was free.

As the carriage rolled away, Rachel turned to her father. "I am not going to marry Oliver Gugenhauf," she stated firmly.

5

Runaway

That night Templeton Buchanan went on the binge of his life. And for the first time, his daughter made no effort to make the round of taverns in search of him.

Locking herself inside her room, Rachel pulled a bundle of letters from a shoebox where she had hidden them. It was not unlike her father to read her mail. His suspicious nature contrived visions of some secret love who might try and "steal my daughter from me." Rachel knew that any love, secret or otherwise, would have been of no consequence provided the young man had financial means to support her father, herself, and himself—in that order.

Of course, the possibility of her leaving had never entered his mind, Rachel was sure. She had a "secret love" all right—the dream of getting away. Just how she would manage, Rachel was never sure. But she did know *where*.

As a child, there had been little time in her secluded life to cultivate friends. Yolanda Lee had been the only girl her own age Rachel regarded as a close personal friend. Both girls were shy by nature and shared each other's dreams of one day meeting and being properly courted by a young man they could love and respect by their high standards. Carefully, they had prepared their list of qualifications, arranging and rearranging them as the years passed. They desired a devout Christian, certainly—and a good citizen, too. Then, each wanted a man of intelligence and, of course, he must be gentle, kind, and *loving*. Eventually *loving* headed the list and secretly Rachel added another qualification all her own: A sense of adventure was essential!

Well, what could offer greater adventure than traveling to the Oregon Territory? Which is what the more fortunate Yolanda did. It happened very suddenly. Rachel still recalled the ache in her heart when, after hearing a speech by a glib-tongued man named Burnett, her friend's parents signed up to go along with one of the first wagon trains.

The man appealed to the patriotism of Eastern folk, painting a colorful picture of the glorious empire they would establish on the Pacific shores.

"With our trusty rifles we shall drive the British back home where they belong!" he promised, making no mention of any hardships along the unblazed trails between the East and West Coasts. Nobody asked and Yolanda made no allusion to problems. Her letters were as glowing as the orator's words. So it must be a relatively easy trip. With just enough trials to furnish a challenge!

As usual, Rachel's hands trembled as she untied the ribbon binding the letters. Yolanda wrote of the gentle climate where soil yielded the richest return imaginable with only the slightest cultivation, where the trees were laden with mellow fruits, where salmon and other fish crowded the sparkling streams, and (Rachel always smiled at this line): "...where the principal labor of the settlers is keeping their gardens free from the inroads of buffalo, deer, elk, and wild turkeys! No more shopping for the Sunday roast!"

Always there had been some restless and adventurous spirit within Rachel Buchanan which even her rowdy father failed to possess. *Were such feelings inherited?* Rachel always wondered.

Her mother recounted stories of her own parents' being among the earliest settlers in Boston. Of fine English lineage, the Boones remained in the city long enough to be entered on the social register and then spread out. The same desires to conquer the unknown that brought them to the Atlantic shores stirred them westward. Some seemed to have been swallowed up by the jaws of the earth, Mother said, while others made it on to Missouri.

Mother never heard from them again, although she sent Rachel many times to ask of the family's whereabouts when scouts would return from their trail-blazing assignments. The frontiersmen would give reports and share their hair-raising experiences which never failed to create a new stir of interest in Rachel.

That stir was enough. If there was a new place to go, the true pioneers wanted to be the first to get there. Rachel understood that about herself and her mother's family. Now in the more modern times of the mid-1800s, Rachel felt that restless stir inside herself to blaze a new trail.

She shivered with excitement at another of Yolanda's letters:

> There's a bill in Congress now to give every Oregon settler a square mile of land, along with a quarter section for each child. If this bill should pass, a family with twelve children would have four square miles. Why, Rachel, we would be rich! There are only eleven of us young ones. But Pa says Ma's good for one more. And she hasn't said, "No." There are as many men here as wild turkeys, all looking for wives!

There were, Yolanda pointed out, a good many "Oregon Trails" now, the spreading out necessary because grass and wild game along the original route were getting scarce. Since the gold strike in California, the situation was a little worse, now and then an unfriendly Indian tribe. And they liked collecting hair, particularly women's.

"Well, I might as well be scalped as stay here and be sold to the highest bidder." Rachel spoke the words aloud, a smile of anticipation curving her mouth.

The smile vanished in an instant. For before her there flashed the vision of Oliver Gugenhauf's hairless skull. The choice Father offered had been no choice at all: She could either marry that deformed dwarf with an onion for a head; or she could—*oh, dear God, no!*—ruin the reputation of an innocent man and die of humiliation. Angry, she had been able to stand up against her father; but now in the quietude of her room, Rachel knew that one way or another her father would manage to manipulate her.

Unless somehow she was able to bring life to the dream of escape harbored in her breast for so long. There was only one possibility and it lay in the wildest fantasy of all—the Oregon Territory! It was ironic that the man whose fate she held in her hands also held her fate in his own.

She must find Colby Lord...warn him...and then ask him to take her with him.

And so it was that Rachel Buchanan became a runaway—only in her mind, but that was a beginning.

6

"Immodest" Request

Dawn was still a pale-yellow promise when Rachel stole out of the house carrying with her the barest essentials and a few mementos. She had no firm plan except to get away before her drunken father returned. Whatever she did must be done discreetly. She shuddered to think of what Father would do if word reached him that his daughter was inquiring about the "scoundrel" to whom he owed so great a sum. Templeton Buchanan would track them down, add their every move to his list of "evidence," then see that they were punished publicly.

How, then, was she to find Colby Lord's whereabouts? Memory of their last meeting made her dread the mission ahead. But instinct told her that he would understand her behavior was due to the mistaken identity. Certainly the embarrassment was nothing compared to what lay ahead. "Please, Lord," she whispered, "please help me with this."

The little fishing village loomed ahead. Buildings, silhouetted between the tentative sunrise and the steely calm of the morning sea, provided a certain protection. Cautiously, Rachel darted from one building to the other, keeping out of sight and hoping to see a friendly face. She knew so few people. *Which ones could she trust?*

A few fishing nets spread out like night-spun cobwebs; but most of the boats were gone. And there were no lights—except in the dread places, the pubs. Those she must avoid at all cost. Maybe this was hopeless. Maybe. . .

Rachel was aware then that something had moved at her left. From the corner of her eye she could make out a human form standing straight and tall in the entrance of the "Water Hole," long arms swinging the half-doors wide open, then letting them swing closed.

A cold, wet fog had blown in to add chill to that which gripped her heart. Pulling her shawl closer to her shivering body, Rachel took a step backward. Then, glancing over her shoulder, she stopped, her heart filled with so many mixed emotions she would never be able to label them all.

"Cole," she whispered, wondering if he could hear her voice above the heavy hammering of her heart. "Cole, I— we—"

But the man she had earlier mistaken for a suitor put a silencing finger to his lips and moved soundlessly toward her. In what seemed like a single fluid motion he was at her side, his broad shoulders shielding her from any prying eyes. And then his strong arms were about her and the two of them were hurrying through the protective mist to the rail where Colby Lord had tethered his stallion.

Before there was time for Rachel to explain the urgency

of her mission, the man had mounted his steed and swept her up in front of him. And then they were galloping away at a speed which pushed her against the familiar strength of his chest. The wet fog loosened her hair and the wind blew it against the face behind her. Her skirts billowed out with the wind's force and to her horror Rachel saw that the worn fabric was slitting to expose her ankles.

Colby looked down and her embarrassment was complete. But, being the gentleman that he undoubtedly was, he did not take advantage of her helpless situation. Instead, he slowed the horse, loosened his own topcoat, and wrapped it about her. That, Rachel realized, was the first act of gentle kindness she had ever known from a man. She owed him an explanation, an offer of help. But the whistle of the wind made conversation impossible. They could talk when they reached their destination. She wondered where that was.

In spite of the possible danger that stalked them, Rachel felt a wild, sweet glow of excitement. Her fear was subsiding, but her heart refused to slow down. It was the adventure of it all, she reasoned. But when the strong arms in which she was held tightened as they came upon a curve, she admitted to herself that being so near Colby Lord made the situation exciting. And wonderful!

Rachel wondered who he was, where he came from, and how he came to lend her shiftless father money. He must be a man of means. So why hadn't her father presented *him* as a prospective husband? The loan, she supposed, would have precluded that. The loan and Cole's integrity. She wondered for the first time what he was doing coming from a pub at that early hour. And, admittedly, she felt a certain pang of disappointment that he frequented such places at all.

But she must concentrate on the problems at hand. Regrettably, there was no time. Through the heavy mists a grove of trees became visible and as Cole reined in, Rachel made out shapes, the likes of which she had not seen before. Some sort of vehicles were they? Wagons? While she pondered the situation, the stallion snorted. Rachel realized then that the wagons—if that's what they were—were surrounded by horses and mules. A few cows looked up inquiringly.

Cole dismounted and helped her down. "Conestogas," he nodded toward the wagons, undoubtedly answering the question in her eyes.

Rachel nodded vaguely. Her sense of urgency made her oblivious to the strangeness of their surroundings. In the distance she heard the laughter of children and the happy barking of dogs as if they were romping together. But all she was able to hear clearly was an inner voice urging her to share the sorry plight which surrounded herself and Cole.

"My father—" she began, reaching out a cold hand to touch Cole's sleeve, "he—he is not a reasonable man—"

Rachel found herself choking on the words. She had known this would be hard. Now, she found it impossible.

To her relief, Cole placed a warm hand over hers. "How well I know!" His laugh was low and pleasant.

Gulping a lungful of air, she tried to go on. "There's no time to waste—hardly time to talk. You must leave at once. If—when he returns and finds me gone—oh, Cole, you *must* go away immediately!"

Cole removed her hand from his and drew her gently to him. She felt warm, secure, and protected. A pleasant languidness crept over her body. Somehow, she must make him understand.

"I—" Rachel was able to get only one word out before bursting into uncontrollable tears.

"There, there, my darling," Cole consoled, pushing the damp curls from her forehead with his broad chin. "You must leave everything to me. Your father, unless I miss my guess, is in no condition to travel. His snores are undoubtedly louder than the giant's in 'Jack and the Beanstalk'! He, as the villagers would say, hung one on last night!"

A sense of weariness stole over her. Cole simply did not understand how quickly her father could recover from his indulgences when there was a need. Any minute now they could be discovered. At the thought, she shivered uncontrollably, causing Cole to draw her closer so that her left ear was against his heart. His compassion and tenderness undid her completely. And, there in the shelter of his arms, she sobbed out the whole story.

Cole rocked her gently back and forth as one would calm a child who has suffered a bad dream. "You poor, poor child. You have been hurt so much. But now maybe between us, the Good Lord and I can heal those wounds."

So Cole was a believer. Oh, she was glad about that! But—and she hoped God understood—there was no time to tell him so. Not until she and Cole had a plan of action.

"You *do* understand?" She looked up at him pitiously.

"How well! I only hope that you do—"

"Oh, I do, Cole! You know I do," Rachel blurted. "But there's something more I have to ask—I mean, I've made you see that you must get away—maybe even without the money he owes you—"

"Yes, I plan on that."

Rachel exhaled in relief and paused. *How could she remain modest and ask the thing of Cole that she must?*

"What more did you wish to ask, Rachel?" he prompted.

"Oh, Cole—I—I—Cole, will you take me with you?"

Cole's arms tightened. "I couldn't leave without you."

7

Strange Bargain

The sun was breaking through the fog, but its hazy glow was out of focus. Rachel felt pleasantly warm. But whether from the struggling beams of sun or the presence of Colby Lord was of no matter anymore. Her world had developed an aura of unreality. Even the words Cole spoke made no sense.

"You're sure you want to leave civilization?"

"It's an uncivilized world I've lived in. You've seen enough to know that. And, *please*, we must get going!"

Cole behaved as if they had all the time in the world.

"I just want to make certain things clear—"

Rachel looked up at him, wondering why he hesitated. A ray of sunlight caught in the depths of his gray-green eyes and there she saw an unreadable message. *Oh, tell me I won't be a burden, Cole—that you want me with you—*

But when he spoke it was to ask if she had thought through what living in the strange, new land would mean. She considered carefully before speaking.

"Well, I can tutor privately. I am good at ciphering and I am considered a good scribe. I know manners and morals—"

Cole shook his head. "That isn't what I meant," he said slowly. "Moreover," he added with a smile, "I'm afraid there will be no such opportunities, Rachel. The settlers do well to establish homes. Tutors would be out of the question. My question was aimed at the adjustments you will be called upon to make—both on the trail and after arrival—"

"Oh, I look forward to that!" Rachel broke in eagerly, her hazel eyes shining.

"I shall pray that shine never leaves your eyes, but I am afraid...well, that remains to be seen. There are matters closer at hand which we must settle—" Cole paused as he was about to say what matters and, with a smile that looked a bit forced, he said, "I am thinking of all those men who wanted your hand in marriage. Are you very sure that not one of them fits the bill?"

Rachel felt herself color. "Oh, how could you ask? I would never, *never*, marry one of those bidders." Her voice rose with indignation, "I would die before marrying a man I could not respect!"

When she saw him wince, Rachel was sorry for her hot words. "Forgive me," she said quickly, her voice filled with remorse. "You have been kind to me. Don't let the fact that I mistook you for someone else stand between us—or the fact that my father has come by the loan in some devious way. At least," she said with a demure smile, "the loan disqualified *you*, saving us both some embarrassment."

"Is that you, Cole?" a motherly-sounding voice called from somewhere among the wagons and animals.

"Yes, Aunt Em—we're coming!" Cole called back. "You'll love her," he promised without further explanation. Then, lowering his voice, he said the words which would linger in her heart forever—bright-winged and fleeting.

"We will be married tonight."

"*Married?*" Rachel stopped breathing.

"Yes," he said simply. And looking at him through the silver curtain of unreality, Rachel wondered how a man's face could look so concerned while in his eyes there was a faint twinkle of something akin to amusement.

"Please—no games." The childlike whisper must be hers.

A slow smile touched his lips. "No games. You have just received a bonafide proposal, my dear. Surely you must have known you could not travel that distance in a party made up largely of men—*alone*? And it would be unthinkable for the two of us to share a companionship without honorable matrimony." The smile died away. "Is the idea so repulsive to you?"

"Oh, no! It's just that I didn't know—didn't realize what I was asking of you—"

Cole waved away her attempt at an explanation. "It is I who proposed. I will ask nothing of you."

"But—but—" Rachel's voice failed her then. Mother had not prepared her to offer herself to a man who asked nothing of a marriage. "I will release you, of course—as soon as the journey is over. And I do owe you so much—" Rachel choked and was unable to go on because of the lump in her throat.

"Oh, Rachel, I would to God that things were different!"

Cole's words came out in a pained groan.

There ought to be something she could say. But what? There was something about his manner that mystified her, something that warned her not to question him.

It was Cole who finally spoke. "It seems fitting and proper that we seal the promise with a kiss—if the lady is willing."

Obediently, Rachel raised her face, turning her cheek demurely to him. Just as obediently, Cole brushed the curve of her cheek with a light kiss. "Now, shouldn't you turn the other cheek?"

Rachel turned the opposite direction and then their eyes caught and held. The same spell of the first meeting was back. Seeming to have no will of her own, Rachel lifted her arms to his neck. Instantly, his lips were on hers. Then, with a little groan, he pushed her away, leaving her senses reeling.

8

"Quiet Wedding"

The woman Cole had addressed at a distance as "Aunt Em" stood in silhouette against the light filtering between an endless line of wagons. Then slowly she began to walk toward them, as if testing the ground to see if it would support her weight.

Rachel watched in detached fascination as the middle-age woman approached, her ample body looking even heavier by the encircling apron over a dark sackcloth dress.

Cole made the proper introductions. Rachel curtsied and

hoped that she made the right responses—uncertain as to what they should be. As yet, she had no idea as to why they were here in this—what was it anyway—a *gypsy camp?* Certainly it was not the environment she would have supposed to be Cole's usual domain.

Talk was flowing around her, but Rachel heard none of the words. Neither could she be sure the man who towered beside her had actually proposed. It had happened too fast, too unexpectedly.

Unable then to deal with past or present, Rachel's mind did a flash-forward: *Tonight is my wedding night. . . I am going to Oregon. . . with Colby Lord.*

Cole must have spoken the same words for Aunt Em had gently gathered Rachel in her arms and was holding her close to the warm bosom. The older woman's rough, work-worn hands pushed straying curls from Rachel's forehead and her gray eyes were moist with tears.

"About time you took a wife for yourself, young man, and such a pretty young thing. Any idea what you're gettin' into, my child?" Aunt Em asked good-naturedly, wiping her eyes in the meantime with the corner of her apron.

No, she didn't, Rachel admitted. Well, yes she did. . . that is, she *thought* she did.

Later she remembered the other woman's soft laugh. Then, with a promise to make the bride beautiful, Aunt Em shooed Cole away.

Aunt Emmaline Galloway had a hard time living up to her promise. There were many interruptions and, although the older woman tried to shield her from prying eyes, it was difficult once word got around that a wedding was taking place "in the grove."

Talk between them was almost impossible. There was so much Rachel needed to know. But how could she ask without telling more about the situation than was safe to reveal? And the woman endeared herself to Rachel by asking no questions. She kindly offered to mend and press Rachel's dress, an offer Rachel couldn't refuse since she had no other garments. Aunt Em left her then, commanding her to rest.

"I understand that both of you're wishin' a quiet wedding?"

When Rachel nodded, Aunt Em smiled, "But I can't be promisin' much peace afterwards. These folks are in a mood to celebrate, you know."

Rachel was too tired to ask the meaning of the words or read anything into them. She simply lay down on the hair mattress in the wagon bed to which the woman directed her and dropped into a dreamless sleep—her first in two days.

Fighting her way back to consciousness, Rachel was dimly aware of being too warm beneath the mackinaw blanket. The clouds had lifted. The golden sun, having completed its work, dropped to the horizon to let the day die in peace, perhaps without the shadows of the past to dim it. Witlessly, she tried to put her thoughts together.

Then she was jolted awake. Something had moved beside her. Cole! He sat at the edge of the wagon bed, his legs drawn up and bound by the wrap-around position of his long arms.

"Oh, Cole—you aren't supposed to see me—it's bad luck—I mean, what day *is* this?"

A light flared in his eyes. "It's still our wedding day; but we've met already today. So my seeing you can't be a bad omen. Aunt Em has warmed your bath. She'll show you which of the wagons serves for milady's toilette. I'm afraid, my dear, you will be finding a lot of inconveniences—"

"Oh, I don't mind! I'm grateful. This is much safer than risking a trip back to the village for the—the ceremony. Where will we meet the wagon train, Cole?"

"Rachel, I'm afraid I have botched this terribly. Forgive

me, but so many things were crowding into my mind. Now, ready yourself for the facts."

His gray-green eyes met hers compellingly and not once did they waver. "Look at me, Rachel—look at me and trust me. Details can come later—"

"But the wagon train—I do need to know where—"

"This *is* the wagon train, Rachel."

Cole spoke quietly and pointed to the wagons her dulled eyes had not seen before. The lettering "FOR OREGON" was painted across their canvas tops.

"When?" she whispered.

"Tomorrow."

Tomorrow! Tomorrow she would be Mrs. Colby Lord and, true to her heritage, striking out for the new frontier. A thrill of excitement ran up and down her backbone. And then the excitement turned to fear.

"Cole," she whispered, trying to disentangle herself from the blanket, "what if my father follows?"

Cole straightened up, then leaned down to pull her to her feet.

"He won't," he promised in a voice of quiet conviction.

The minister, Rachel learned just minutes before the sunset ceremony, was Aunt Em's husband, David Galloway, also known as "Brother Davey." Rachel hardly heard the little man's sparse words. When Cole placed a gold ring with an enormous diamond on her trembling hand, she failed to note its shimmering beauty or hear him say that it had belonged to his mother.

All too quickly it was over. Rachel Buchanan had become the wife of Colby Lord, whom she hardly knew.

But there was no time to think. The music of violins, flutes, and accordions joined the wind song of the night. The soon-to-be-travelers were more like revelers. Were they really this excited over a wedding?

Aunt Em, seeing the lost look on her face, came to stand beside Rachel.

"They're always light of heart the night before the start," she confided. "Most likely 'tis to hide their worry."

If that was intended to put my concerns to rest, the words missed their target, Rachel thought. *What could they be so afraid of—unless they somehow knew of Father's wrath?*

The singing and dancing commenced then, and Rachel found herself caught up in their festive mood in spite of the strange circumstances.

Cole, engaged in conversation with a cluster of other men, signaled to her several times. When at last he joined her, Rachel smiled in appreciation. Her feet hurt and emotionally she was drained.

"Is this really what one would call a 'quiet wedding'?" she inquired with a smile.

Cole squeezed her hand and laughed in the low, deep way she was coming to love so much.

"It hardly qualifies, does it? But it is 'quiet' in the sense that your father would hardly think of looking for us here. And now off to bed you go—"

Rachel felt her heart skip a beat. *Bed!*

They had not discussed sleeping arrangements, but she had supposed that he understood. She found herself praying for direction...and time for the proper response.

As if in answer to her prayer, the minister joined them. First, he offered his congratulations. Then he added his best wishes.

When he continued to linger, Cole, with a little side wink at Rachel, commented soberly, "Well, Brother Davey, I do believe I forgot to pay you, sir."

David Galloway traced a circular motion on the ground in front of him.

"Makes no never mind, I assure you—no never mind a-tall. Just you pay me whatever you think she's worth!" he teased.

Rachel felt her heart turn over and then drop to the toes

of her pointed shoes. For a single moment she raised stricken eyes to her husband.

Then, with a little heartbroken cry, she ran to hide herself behind the nearest wagon. And there she sobbed until there were no tears left inside her.

9

Abandoned Bride

At last, spent and weary, Rachel lifted her head from against the canvas covering of the wagon. Wagging her head from side to side to clear it, she was unaware of the angelic vision she presented when her golden hair tumbled down her shoulders in loose array.

She was unaware of anything except the tangled web which she had woven—only to become its captive. Her fear had turned to sadness. . .a sadness that went too deep for healing with the balm of tears. How long, she wondered, could she bear the burden of being a "for-sale-or-trade" item—only to compound matters by offering *herself?*

Would she always smart under the slightest allusion to "worth" as she had beneath the words spoken in jest by Brother Davey? Would they reject her, think her immodest, when the kind people she was to travel with found out the awful truth?

In that state of anxiety, Rachel did not sense another person was nearby until a quick, effortless motion brought her husband to her side.

"How long have you been here?" Rachel gasped, making an unsuccessful swipe at her tear-stained face.

"All the time."

Cole's voice was gentle. "I will always be here whenever you need me, Rachel. You must believe that. But there are times when the presence of another is an intrusion."

He fished in his pocket for a handkerchief and handed it to Rachel. When she thanked him, he gave her a little lopsided grin.

"For what?"

"For understanding just now . . . " Rachel paused to blow her nose. "For lending me your handkerchief . . . for marrying me . . . "

Cole groaned and reached to take her in his arms; but Rachel pulled away, lest she be robbed of her own will. This was a business arrangement and she must be careful to put Cole in no worse circumstance than that which she had imposed on him already.

Arms dangling at his sides, Cole addressed her in a voice sounding almost sad.

"You're thanking me for trifles, Rachel. There is no need for that, believe me!" Then, inhaling deeply, he said, "As to marrying you—any man in his right mind would recognize his treasure. It is *I* who am grateful—much more grateful and humbled than you will ever know."

Maybe he was right in some small sense of the word. She

supposed his pride had been saved, his reputation, perhaps even his life. But she had personally sacrificed nothing, while Cole had given up his very freedom for her. She would try to make it all up to him, be a good wife—not in the total sense of the word—but a good *domestic* wife. Fleetingly, Rachel wondered how they would keep up appearances. Marriage wasn't something a wife could spread on herself like buttering bread...but...

"Aunt Em will show you to our wagon," Cole said suddenly. "She will help you prepare for bed and I will look in on you later. Why are you trembling, Rachel?"

His voice flowed around her, like music from the fiddles and flutes, to lodge somewhere in the area of her heart. Darkness had settled about them, bringing its inevitable sense of intimacy. A strange sense of longing filled Rachel's heart—one she must put aside quickly. She could not control her desires, but she *could* control her emotions.

A soft night breeze, scented with the first breath of spring, caressed her cheek. Then, playfully, it lifted her hair. The hand Rachel lifted to smooth her long locks was still shaking as she remembered Cole's question.

"Yes, I suppose we should get inside. There's a chill to the air. Will the snows be melted in the mountains?"

Cole was turning toward a halo of light which seemed to be coming their direction.

"Aunt Em—with a candle," he said. "And to answer about the snow, scouts say the trails are passable now. Aunt Em, here we are. Will you show my bride to the marriage chambers?"

"Be off with you now!" Aunt Em's cheery voice blended with Cole's soft laugh as he turned away and disappeared in the darkness. "Marriage chambers, indeed! That Cole is a teasin' one—but, oh, such a gentleman, he is. He's started this trip—let me see—three times or is it four counting when he planned on takin' *her*...but this is no time for small talk. Come along, dearie."

Rachel had halted in the dark, however. Her shock

was overwhelming. There were so many details she didn't know. It had never occurred to her that he might be married—or that he planned to be or had been.

"Aunt Em!" Rachel's voice sounded hollow and distant. She swallowed, but the lump in her throat remained. "Aunt Em, is Cole—is he married—I mean, you said it was time he took a wife—and, oh, I'm afraid I'm confused—"

"Now, now." The older woman's fleshly arms were about Rachel's slender body, the candle held precariously close to her back. "We all feel confused and sort of jumpy on our weddin' night. 'Twouldn't be normal otherwise."

Gingerly, she lifted the hand holding the candle over Rachel's head and held it in front of them. Then with the free arm around Rachel, she gently pushed her forward.

In the dimness of the candlelight the wagon Aunt Em stopped before looked like a tent. She pushed aside the canvas flaps and entered from the back. Then, lighting a larger candle from the one she carried, the kindly woman said, "Yours is one of the biggest and best of the caravan, Rachel. Cole's better off than most. Come see what he's done for your weddin' present!"

"I never thought of a gift," Rachel whispered. "I have no trousseau, no dowry—"

"It's little I know of such matters, my child," Aunt Em exclaimed as she laid out a collection of simple, but beautifully-made, calico dresses and matching bonnets. "I say, will you look at these?" She bent to bite off a thread, "And *this!*"

Rachel stared but words failed her. Undoubtedly, the nightgown and matching robe were practical cotton; but in the candle's pale glow they were a gossamer mist of sheerest silk. Fascinated, she watched as Aunt Em turned back a brightly-embroidered comforter. Then tactfully the older woman backed out of the wagon.

Rachel snuffed out the candle. In the velvet blackness she changed from the threadbare dress into the soft night garment and brushed her hair, counting the strokes to synchronize with the heavy pounding of her heart. The pounding continued as she knelt beside the mattress on the floor and whispered, "Lord, I need You as never before. I know Your requirements for a good wife. Help me be one."

Her prayer was interrupted by Cole's voice just outside the wagon, saying softly, "Good night, Rachel."

She felt relieved—but abandoned.

10

♥

"Farewell, My Love"

Outside, the waning moon rose, hovered palely, and then—as if it had waited long enough—slid downward. Inside the tent, the young bride sobbed into her feather pillow. *I'll never understand you, Rachel Buchanan—I mean Rachel LORD. How could you wish him gone, then wish him back?* she whispered miserably to herself.

Vaguely, she remembered seeing several muskets standing in a front corner of the wagon—maybe for bagging game, maybe for possible battle. But the greatest battle was within herself.

Rachel was still wide awake when a bugle call split the silence. Cautiously, she crawled to peek through the flaps serving as curtains at the back of the wagon. It was still pitch dark, so dark that she bumped heads with another human being. With a startled cry, she crawfished backward only to see that someone was following.

Then suddenly it was all right. "Oh, Cole!"

"If I frightened you, I am sorry." Cole reached to take her hand in the darkness. "I'll light a candle—"

"Oh, no! I mean—you can't—I'm not dressed!"

Rachel, aware that she was babbling, reached out to pluck at his coat sleeve. At the same time, she fumbled for the robe he had provided. The fabric of the gown felt as thin as morning mist and by candlelight it would be transparent.

"Oh, Rachel, Rachel," Cole was laughing as he lighted the candle, "I am your husband, remember? I ask nothing of you. Remember that, too. But wouldn't it look a bit strange for the bride and groom to emerge from separate wagons?"

Having located the robe, Rachel pulled it about her quickly. It occurred to her then that he had said "separate wagons."

"Do you have two—wagons, I mean?"

"Not wives?" he teased and and must have wondered at the quick flush the words brought to her cheeks. "Yes, two wagons," Cole said, sobering, "plus some stock and cattle and Moreover—the hound."

"More-over?" Rachel repeated, dividing the words. "That's a *name*?"

A buzz of voices rose from outside and the air filled up with the tantalizing smell of wood smoke, bacon, and coffee. Rachel realized then that she was ravenously hungry. She was unable to remember when she had last eaten. She sniffed appreciatively.

"Do that again." His words were almost a caress. "The way you wrinkle your funny little nose makes you look like a baby rabbit—lost, scared, and heart-winning. But you best get dressed, my little bunny. We hit the trail before the roosters are awake."

With that, he pulled himself to as much of a standing position as the low arch of the wagon bows would allow and hunched toward the door. The robe slipped from Rachel's shoulders as Cole turned to dismount. She stooped to recover it, holding it protectively against her and lowering her gaze.

A look of amusement shone in his eyes, but Cole's voice was matter-of-fact when he spoke.

"Brother Davey named the dog," he answered in response to her previous question. "Says it was meant to be. Seems his puppyhood tongue was what healed a small cut on the good man's finger. Brother Davey likes to quote the passage from St. Luke: '. . . moreover the dogs came and licked his sores.' " He chuckled. "No amount of talk's going to convince him that *Moreover* wasn't a name. And you'll find the reverend takes some liberties here and there with other Scriptures, too."

Rachel laughed with him and then Cole was gone. Quickly, she dressed and climbed out of the wagon, following the titillating breakfast smells to a bonfire. There a man heaped a mountain of food onto a tin pan and handed it to her without looking up.

Cole stepped from the outer rim of the morning-dark to stand by her side. But, before they could engage in any sort of conversation, all was in confusion. A youngish man named Julius Doogan was trying to explain the route. At the same time, Brother Davey was insisting that the food (even that which had been consumed) must be blessed. Each was endeavoring to outtalk the other, neither being successful.

Children, interrupted from their sleep, were crying and the cows bellowed incessantly. "Needin' to be milked!" a woman named Agnes Grant explained loudly. Then, when somewhere in the distance a rooster crowed, the woman shook her head. "Bad sign," she said darkly.

People began climbing into their wagons as some of the men watered down the fire. Those in their wagons were anxious to be off; but still Julius Doogan and Brother Davey stood toe-to-toe, their noses almost touching, engrossed in a debate as to whether the wagon train would follow a leader (Mr. Doogan) or "where the spirit led" (the preacher).

"I supposed they would be much better organized," Rachel said to nobody in particular, then regretted the words. Who could be more disoriented than she?

She sought Cole's eyes for a signal as to what she should do; but Cole was mounting a box and raising his hand for silence. To her surprise, the crowd obliged and when he spoke, they listened. Rachel listened, too, with a thrill of pride.

"All right, folks! This is it, the day we've been waiting for—the day we leave *together*. Divided, we cannot stand. Now listen to the order from Doogan—and tonight," he promised Brother Davey, "they'll listen to *you*. May the Lord make His face to shine upon you all . . . until we meet in St. Jo!"

A shout rose up from the crowd, but it could not drown out the words Rachel had heard. *St. Jo?* That would be St. Joseph, Missouri. The wagon train was going that direction . . . perhaps to meet up with other travelers. But did she understand her husband would not be among them? She had never felt so alone.

With her heart heavy inside her, Rachel allowed herself to be propelled back to the wagon by Cole's strong hands, hands she could not do without. Oh, how did he think she could manage? Why hadn't he told her?

Cole was speaking. She must listen. "I regret that business will detain me, Rachel—"

"Not my father? Oh, not my father, Cole!"

"Not your father," he said positively. "I will join you in St. Joseph . . . and then we will do some long overdue talking. Aunt Em will drive this wagon; Brother Davey, the other."

Then, suddenly, she was in his arms. "Farewell, my love," he said sadly. And then he was gone.

11

Along the Trail

Sunrise. Sunset. The days took on a sameness. The wagons seemed to gain only a few miles between. Rachel would always remember the confusion of the first day. Children and dogs trotted alongside the wagons excitedly for the first few hours, then grew weary and quarrelsome. The cattle, not yet conditioned to moving ahead, wandered away in search of grass. Adults, not yet bothered by hint of hardship and danger ahead, were eager and unfatigued. So, in spite of the confusion, Rachel felt herself caught up in the mystery of it all.

As Rachel climbed into the wagon to sit beside Aunt Em that first day out, Agnes Grant muttered that chances of "getting through were a hundred to one against the possibility." At which the capable Emmaline Galloway clucked her tongue.

"There'll always be women like Aggie, I'm guessin'— them that are natural-born complainers and meddlers. 'Sorrow Birds' I call 'em. And I think the Good Lord knows they come by the name rightly!"

Rachel smiled. Already, she had grown to appreciate the woman who was to drive Cole's wagon. Here was a person to be trusted, someone in whom she could confide, and certainly a wise adviser.

"I'm so glad Cole brought us together. I have so much to learn about traveling—about life—and *him*—"

Aunt Em laughed heartily. "Can't bring yourself to say *husband* yet, can you, dearie? Well, let me tell you that the man you've married is a fine one. Giddyup, Napoleon!"

Napoleon? Rachel, wondering whether the draft animal's name came from the conqueror or the filled French pastry she was so fond of, smiled. She was finding more to smile about these days. Or was she simply learning to smile?

"Go ahead—ask away." The older woman's eyes twinkled as she turned away from the team to look at Rachel. "I know more about Colby Lord than those who'll be tellin' it different."

Rachel considered the strangeness of the words then decided against comment. Instead, she asked timidly, "How old is he—my husband?"

"Older'n you by a good six years, I'd judge—and he's done a lot of livin' in them twenty-six years. Time's not always dealt kindly with Cole—his mother and older brother bein' killed like that left him pretty dead inside." Aunt Em paused to look quizzically at Rachel. "I can see he's told you nothin'. . .but, then, you've been allowed precious little time together, poor lambs. The killin' was a result of the stand against slavery Colby's father took—him and a handful of neighbors. Know your history?"

Rachel nodded. "I know about the slave uprising that followed...but what did that have to do with Cole's mother and brother?"

"Sure you've a stomach for this?" Rachel wasn't sure, but she wanted to hear, so she nodded again.

"They—both of 'em—was, what's the word for gettin' your head removed?"

"Decapitated?" Rachel whispered in horror. *Poor Cole!*

"That's the word! Come on, Napoleon, show them mules what you can do!" The woman's order came out uncertainly, as if she were trying to encourage herself as well as the team. "Folks said it was the slaves who did the—the slaughterin', but everybody knew it was a get-even tactic of the dirty politicians. Virginia was goin' through a depression; but Cole wasn't one of the 'no-shoes-poor' young'uns. Mr. Lord provided well—a trader dealing in foreign goods, had a big fleet of floatin' vessels—"

Rachel felt her shoulders slump with sheer fatigue, all strength gone, even though they had been on the road only a part of one day. Sleep tugged at her eyelids, but she fought it away and rallied enough to ask what became of Cole's father.

Aunt Em clucked to the team, then praised them for picking up speed before answering.

"Pirates," she said at last. "They came aboard somewhere in the China seas—killed all the crew—and word has it, tossed Captain Lord and young nephew Elton overboard and watched the drownin'. There, now, I've upset you, and all the while I was only wishin' to make you understand—"

"You have helped—truly, you have," Rachel managed to say, although her heart quailed within her. "Cole knows something of my background—" she paused, wishing she had not drawn attention to herself, "so," she went on doggedly, "it is good that I know something of his. Do you mind if I ask what he does for a living now?"

Emmaline Galloway's face relaxed in a smile. "It is all right to ask anything you wish to know about a body's mate! Well, now, you pay no attention to the talk—just trust him. He's as honest as the day is long . . . which reminds me, we'll be pitchin' camp for the night right soon. Most likely," she surmised, glancing at the lowering sun, "Mr. Doogan's lookin' for a stream."

Yes, of course, they would need water. Rachel wondered aloud how they would manage going across the deserts. Aunt Em didn't "rightly know." The parson was a "travelin' man," but his "calls" had never taken him so far before.

Stiffly, Rachel climbed from the wagon two hours later. She longed to lie down but was advised to take a brisk walk to work off the stiffness. She walked westward, thinking of all she had learned that day about Colby Lord . . . and wishing she knew more.

12

What Do Women Look For?

In the days that followed, Rachel grew more and more curious about her husband. He was, as Aunt Em insisted, "a true gentleman." Or so it seemed in their first encounter. And surely he must be a kind man, doing what he did to rescue her from some fateful marriage; patient, too, else he would have foreclosed on the mortgage, taken their home, and put them out on the streets. *But how*, she wondered, *had he reckoned with Father? What had detained him on the day the wagon departed? And what did he do for a living? Did I only imagine a tightening of Emmaline Galloway's mouth when questioned as to the nature of Cole's business?* Here was a true friend, one who was fiercely loyal.

Aunt Em's high regard served to elevate Cole even higher in Rachel's mind...but the nagging questions persisted. Well, she must discipline herself to put away any doubts. She owed it to him to be a good mistress on the trail, even though she was not a true wife.

What Colby Lord was or was not was really of no consequence. By agreement, they would be parting at the end of this journey—or so her mind said. Her heart told her something quite different. So, by day, she questioned his loyal friend. And, by night, she directed almost all her prayers to her husband's safety, asking that her words and deeds might be acceptable in the Lord's sight and that her behavior be acceptable in the eyes of her husband.

Lost in thought on one of the endless days since the party of twelve wagons had headed west, Rachel was startled when Aunt Em said she hoped they would be neighbors in the new homeland. "But then I guess you young folks will be preferrin' the city—settin' yourselves up in business." Her sigh said that she and Brother Davey would not.

Rachel pondered the question. "I don't know exactly what Cole plans," she said slowly. Realizing that most married couples would have planned these things together, she hurried on. "I know so little about the new land—other than that I want to go. I've wanted to see the Oregon Territory since my friend began a flow of glowing letters about its wild beauty—'unspoiled,' she calls it."

Emmaline Galloway wiped perspiration from her forehead and adjusted her sunbonnet. "Unspoiled, yes—unspoiled and un*tamed*. I'm supposin' you wrote you'd be comin'?"

"There wasn't time," Rachel answered and could have bitten her tongue.

But if Aunt Em noticed anything amiss, she gave no indication of it. Without a change of expression, she nodded.

"A whirlwind romance was it now? Well, the Almighty knows His business in bringin' the right folks together. Why, I remember how 'twas when me and my Davey laid eyes on one 'nother. Kind of shy 'round women-folk, he was, but me—I knew a good man when I saw one..." Aunt Em paused to laugh, then she went on in a conspiratory voice, "I was just thinkin' what a rich morsel this would give Aggie's gossip-lovin' tongue—my up and poppin' the question when he poked 'round."

Rachel felt the blood drain from her face as she lifted a hand to her mouth to stifle a little sob. *Is every word spoken by another destined to be a painful reminder of how I came to be the wife of Colby Lord?*

"Are you all right?" Aunt Em was asking. "Want I should rein in somewheres near? You've been peckin' at your food like a canary—and chances are you've not even slept a wink, being apart from your husband and all."

"I'm all right—really I am," Rachel assured her, pretending to smooth a wrinkle from the dusty folds of her long, full skirt. Stopping would cause more curiosity than was already rampant. She owed it to Cole to show composure, saying nothing that would cause him embarrassment.

The two women were silent for a time. Rachel tried to get a view of the countryside, but the dust stirred up by the wagons ahead reduced visibility to nothingness. Her mouth felt as dry as the cracked earth beneath the feet of the mule team. Although it was spring, this part of the world seemed to have tasted no rain. She wondered why no houses were in view, then began sensing the vastness of the New World—smiling at the thought of being an "explorer" and the next moment shuddering at the loneliness. Cole would be about his business, whatever it was. Undoubtedly, David and Emmaline Galloway would keep moving. And she would be all alone...

It was Aunt Em who broke the silence. Her words had nothing to do with what Rachel was thinking; but she welcomed the sound of a familiar voice above the rumble of the wagon wheels.

"Awful hot, considerin' it's spring. Mules are in a lather—why, they'll be done in before we meet up with t'others. You knew the party'd be bigger?" The woman wiped her red face.

"I surmised as much," Rachel said. "You know, the way Yolanda spoke of the Applegate Trail, I thought there would be oxen instead of mules."

Aunt Em nodded. "There will be soon as we hit St. Jo and rest up a spell. Come on, boys, you can make it up this little hump," she encouraged the team. Then, as if remembering, "Who's Yolanda? Somebody meetin' you in St. Jo?"

"Oh, no, nobody's meeting me. I'll be all alone—"

" 'Cepting for your husband—that's hardly bein' alone, now is it?"

"Of course not—I mean, I *know* nobody else. I'm hoping, as you are, that you will settle near me—us." And, then, afraid that her constant slips of the tongue revealed that something was wrong, she hurried on. "Yolanda is my friend in the Oregon Territory. We were always best friends—you know, the kind you swing with and share confidences. Why, I remember the lists we compiled as to what our husbands should be like," Rachel said with a laugh.

"That's healthy enough," Aunt Em said. "We women are dreamers, you know. Sometimes I wonder if we meet the man who fits the mold or if we stuff him inside it—" Her voice trailed off.

Rachel found herself wondering if the older woman was happy or accepted life's trials without ever asking herself whether she had found happiness. At any rate, the woman possessed a wisdom that she hoped to gain. Maybe it was the strangeness of new life she was entering that gave Rachel the courage to ask Emmaline Galloway so personal a question.

"Aunt Em, what did *you* look for in a husband?"

To her surprise, the older woman became noticeably flustered.

"Me? I—why, what most women look for I'll be guessin'. Seems to me a man ought to be a good provider—and it's pretty nice if men can make us laugh now and then . . . and me now—"

She paused to tighten the reins as the team reached the top of the little hill and began to pick up speed in descent. "You'll be wantin' to learn how to drive a wagon, I expect, as well as the kind of cookin' that goes with this kind of journey. I'll be helpin' you. It'll be every feller—or I should say *fam'ly*—for hisself once we head out from Missoura."

Rachel listened, a little knot tightening in her stomach at the words. As a loyal wife, even though it was in name only and of her own doing, she must learn . . . but how better than to know something about the man she was married to? She felt that Aunt Em would go back to their previous conversation.

And she was right. "Me, like I was sayin'—I don't like a frivolous man who forgets he's married ev'ry time he sees a pretty face . . . and I don't like 'em who are weak and mealymouthed. They oughta be able to speak their piece—in their homes and elsewhere. And, of course, any woman likes bein' courted. My, my, how I do talk! Now, let's talk about you and Yolanda. What're you younger ones lookin' for?"

Rachel smiled and went over the qualifications as she remembered them. They were not too different, the two women agreed.

"Except," Rachel said slowly, "that I put respect at

the top of my list—that is, after full dedication to the Lord."

Aunt Em considered for a moment, then said, "Seems to me that would come naturally if he had all the rest. Cole's your man!"

13

Faith Leads UP—Not Out!

Sometime during the trek Aunt Em began to share the quarters of what she called "Cole's Wagon Number Two" with Rachel at night—an arrangement which pleased Rachel more than she cared to admit. She could cope with the choking dust and the rough jostle of the days. Night was another matter. Then, no matter how fervent her prayers, Rachel could imagine wild animals or Indians prowling around the wagon. She gave no thought to the possibility of other men in the party forcing their way through the canvas flaps, even though Cole had cautioned her. In her mind, she had left all evil-minded men back there with her father. These men were busy, purposeful, and—as far as she could tell—honorable.

But Aunt Em wasn't so sure. "You bein' so pretty and all's 'nough to turn a man's head, dearie. While I envy your innocence, I want to be guardin' it for Cole. Besides which, you're not sleepin'—"

Together the two women read aloud from their Bibles and together they knelt in prayer before extinguishing the candle. And on occasion, before sleep forced their travel-weary eyelids to submit to slumber, they talked.

On one such night Rachel asked Aunt Em concerning the position of her husband's wagon in the procession, Cole's "Wagon Number One." *Did that mean he was in the lead?* No, that "know-it-all" Mr. Doogan was ahead, which seemed to keep the rivalry between the two men alive and healthy. Oh, bother! Maybe 'twas just as well. That gave Agnes something to think on without pesterin' the rest of the folks.

Would there be trouble? Rachel wondered.

"Oh, no, no real trouble," Aunt Em said with assurance. "I never worry about my Davey. He shuts up before breakin' a commandment—sometimes just under the wire, I'd be sayin'. Still, havin' no young'uns of our own," she said with just a hint of sadness, "he sort of takes on the father role. And in this case, it don't seem to be to Mr. Doogan's likin'." She paused to laugh and then pulled herself up on her elbow to share the joke with Rachel.

"First off, young Doogan said, 'Now, parson, I want you to know that no psalm singer's goin' to preach to me along this trail. I'm no candidate.' And my husband said, 'Don't you go worryin'. 'Course you're not. Seein' as how you missed bein' a *human* by a smatterin'!' "

Rachel smiled in the darkness. That the Galloways had a happy marriage she had no doubt. What was the key? In his wife's eyes, Brother Davey possessed all she had looked for in a husband. But there was something else. A kind of understanding between them, the kind born of sharing life's laughter and its tears...and, literally, paying little attention to the morrow, just letting the day be sufficient unto itself. Was that what it took to be a pioneer woman—the ability to shrug off tomorrow and its needs?

But that created a new need! "I need more faith," Rachel said suddenly, hardly aware that she spoke aloud.

Emmaline Galloway took no notice of the words spoken out of context. "You've aplenty. The Almighty saw to that. All His children have to do is be sure the faith given them's aimed the right direction. Me and my Davey don't worry about findin' a way *out*—just a way *up* for folks."

"Thank you, Aunt Em." Rachel touched the older woman's hand in appreciation for her homespun wisdom.

Feeling at peace, Rachel was about to cross the invisible line between wakefulness and slumber when a sudden thought came. "*Moreover!*" she said. "I should have been watching out for him. Do you have any idea where he is?"

"Why, with Davey, of course. Won't leave his master's jacket. Most loyal critter ever I saw. So you sleep, dearie."

Rachel slept. And there came to her a vision of a man with gray-green eyes, shining with love. With outstretched arms he drifted toward her. "Believe in me," he whispered. "Have faith."

14

♥

Reunion

Rachel awoke with a feeling of excitement. After supper around the campfire the previous night, Mr. Doogan announced that they would arrive in St. Jo late the afternoon of the following day. Children squealed. Their parents applauded loudly. And, without invitation, men produced their accordions, flutes, and violins. There was dancing followed by hymns and prayers. Rachel slipped quietly away from the celebration, letting herself blend with the shadows, and retired to the wagon. She was trying to roll her hair on rags the way Mother had taught her when Aunt Em joined her.

"I feel so untidy, so disheveled and unacceptable," she mumbled, trying to hold one of the muslin strips between her teeth as she twisted a self-willed lock of golden hair. "We'll be meeting new people—and I look so beggarly—"

Aunt Em gave her a knowing look. "Yes, you'll want to look your best—though it's hard to imagine your not bein' acceptable to *him*."

Rachel blushed and, with face averted, struggled on with her hair. "I'm sure it will take Cole some time to join us. We got a head start and—*ouch!*" She had jerked at her hair harder than she intended.

Aunt Em began to unstrap her practical high-top shoes. "Oh, he'll be ridin' his stallion, Hannibal. Rides like the wind, you know."

Yes, Rachel knew. And remembering caused her blush to deepen as her heart picked up tempo.

"I've been thinkin', 'a course," Aunt Em's voice was muffled as she tugged at the skirt she was pulling off over her head, "that I'll be returnin' to the other wagon—"

"Oh, no—I mean, that's unnecessary." Rachel gasped for breath and then rushed on, "What I'm saying is that perhaps this is a wise arrangement—you and me—"

Aunt Em spoke from behind her, her words coming slowly as if chosen with care. "It's very necessary, Rachel. You newlyweds need your privacy." She walked to stand in front of Rachel and looked straight into her eyes. "Gettin' a marriage off on the right foot's most important." She held up a hand to silence any protest Rachel might have made. "Like I told you, the Lord never saw fit to bless me with children, so I forthwith take you as my daughter! Now," she said with a touch of gentleness, "I can *order* you to shed your shyness and be the happy bride of the man so dear to me. Besides, it's high time I was crawlin' back in bed with one Brother Davey!"

Rachel had trouble sorting out her feelings after Aunt

Em's even breathing said she was asleep. She was subdued to the point of apprehension by the other woman's pointed comments. It was hard to think of a solution . . . and then, with contradiction, she found herself wishing it were unnecessary. At first, she struggled with such thoughts, feeling them to be unwholesome. And then, it was as if a thousand lights exploded inside her. At last Rachel acknowledged what she must have known all along somewhere deep inside. She must be in love with her husband!

And now, although dawn was some two hours away, she awoke with a pounding heart. Outside there was a gentle stirring which said the others were wakening, too. Quickly pulling on the clean clothes she had laid out the night before, Rachel was about to rouse Aunt Em when she realized that the other woman was gone. *How on earth am I going to manage the long row of buttons down the back of the calico dress?*

Clutching the garment to hide the gap in back, she eased furtively from the wagon toward where she supposed Brother Davey stopped Cole's other wagon for the night. She halted suddenly when there was a touch of a hand on her shoulder in the darkness.

"It's just me," a woman's voice whispered from behind her.

"Mrs. Grant!" Rachel breathed with relief. "I was looking for Aunt Em. I need help with these buttons."

The woman's birdlike hands clawed at the gap in Rachel's dress, further exposing her body. "Come here to the light. I can button as good at that woman."

Rachel had little choice but to walk with her the few remaining steps to the Grant wagon. "You'll be choosin' t'look yer best in St. Jo. Talk 'as it your husband'll be meetin' up with you there. Seems queer-like to most of t'others he taken off like that on your weddin' night and all. If it was *my* husband—"

Irritated, Rachel rushed to Cole's defense. "Mr. Lord had business that needed attending," she said formally.

Agnes Grant fumbled with a button—a delaying tactic, Rachel was sure. " 'Course in business like his'n, I guess a wife 'as t' 'spect anythin'. Right?"

"Wrong!" Rachel said coldly. She would tell this busybody nothing. "Would you mind hurrying, Mrs. Grant?"

The woman resumed the buttoning. "I just don't want no abuse comin' to you 'cause 'a his doin's—past or present. It would be a tragedy—a real tragedy—if'n history repeated itself. I'm talkin' 'about the girl he was marryin'. . . "

Rachel tore herself from Mrs. Grant's hands, unconcerned that the top buttons gaped open. Her head was roaring and her heart was pounding unmercifully. She was angry and at the same time filled with misgivings. There was a growing ache in her bosom.

And then her eyes caught sight of a tall, slender-hipped, broad-shouldered man, silhouetted before the campfire. Only one man in the world possessed such a handsome physique. She ran to her husband in wild abandon.

15

Westward Ho!

Outside St. Joseph, Missouri, a city of tents had mushroomed. Occupants seemed to flock in from all over the world. Rachel, who had expected a commonality dating back to her Pilgrim forefathers, instead found people of diverse personality, race, tongue, and purpose. Only one motive tied them together—a purpose which became their watchword: the words WESTWARD HO!

All were eager to be off, but there was a delay to rest the teams, secure wagon wheels and tongues, and lay in supplies: dried fruit, bacon, dry beans, wheat flour, cornmeal. Rachel looked at the mountains of staples and wondered how one could create a palatable meal. *Well, Aunt Em will help me. And when we reach Oregon, there will never, ever be another problem with food in that gentle climate. In such a land, surely other problems can be resolved, too.* Rachel held fast to her dreams, even as the bickering went on around her:

"I refuse to leave here without Ma's walnut dresser."

"But, don't you be knowin', wife, that sacks of grain's more important?"

"Put an extra barrel on behind, Hank, fer waterin' Grandma's moss rose."

"Now, all them barrels gotta be used fer seed-grain!"

"These books go 'er *I* don't. Want yer childrun growin' up knowin' nothin'?"

"Book larnin's no good without food in our bellies. What ye think the cows'll be eatin' 'crost the way?"

A few doubts began to cloud the rosy horizon of Rachel's mind. She had been buried so deep in her own problems that her thoughts simply had not included others and their quandaries. She wondered for the first time what was responsible for the migration which seemed to be growing larger by the hour.

She had not seen Cole since that emotional meeting by the campfire. Words had seemed unnecessary with his arms around her. They would have plenty of time for talking, only the time had not come and as far as she could determine, Cole made no great effort to avail himself. She, on the other hand, had behaved as if she were available on any terms! That wasn't true. It simply was *not* true! As grateful as she was to Cole for taking her away from her joyless existence, Rachel decided she should be a little more careful, a little more on guard lest her love for him show.

During the three-day layover in St. Joseph, Rachel scarcely caught sight of her husband. He was busy helping new arrivals repack or he was always caucusing with a group of other men, their heads bent over a map. At night, to prevent looting, the men took turns at keeping watch. Rachel suspected that Cole was with them most of the time and once she was sure he was carrying a gun.

Was there really a need for weapons? When she asked Aunt Em, the reply was understandable. "We don't be knowin' what there's a need for, do we, dearie?"

Could Aunt Em use a gun? Rachel asked, wondering if women in the West were expected to hunt for game like the Indian squaws she had read about. Aunt Em had laughed. "All in good time. Huntin' bein' like lookin' for a good man—takes some time and practice." Rachel agreed.

Gradually, once she saw that most of the travelers were as uncertain as she herself was concerning the journey ahead, Rachel moved from tent to tent to introduce herself. To her surprise the women seemed to know Cole and, if they did not know who she was already, they were happy to make her acquaintance. Rachel wondered anew what her husband's business was and what was taking him West.

She pondered these things in her own heart, making no mention of them. Instead, she listened to the stories of their plights and was thankful that nobody asked of hers.

A sad-faced young mother who was nursing twins said that she and her husband had come from the Mississippi Valley—no doctors and everybody dying of ague, winters cold and summers hot, cockleburs taking over the croplands, and streams so sluggish they furnished no food but suckers.

Mandy Burnside, whose husband raised "hawgs," had been forced to sell a whole steamboat load of "sow belly" for less than a hundred dollars. . .the fat pork being used for the boat's fuel.

Land was "tired and pore," Liz Farnall said. Her husband, Mitch, "jest up and walked off'n it. No need in tryin' to sell to them what's got no money. Yep, there was reason 'nuf to go to Orygone," the woman declared.

Each of the women Rachel visited thanked her as if she

had shown them a great kindness. At the time she gave the matter no thought; but somewhere in back of her mind there was a growing conviction that there was a lot of work to be done here. Backgrounds of the other women were totally different from her own; but they had one thing in common: They were *women*. And something told her that they would all have need of one another before reaching the new territory.

Then on the night before departure, Cole's schedule allowed him a moment with her—not much, but enough for her to cling to . . . and ponder over.

Drawing her aside, he put his arms around her gently. "I was proud of you and the way you greeted me, Rachel. That should erase any doubt from Agnes Grant's suspicious mind!"

16

Departure

Long after she had snuffed out the candle, Rachel lay awake in the stuffy darkness of the wagon. Cole had not bothered to put up a tent for them, although once they were on the trail he would pitch camp as the others did.

The April air outside was balmy, touched faintly with the scent of distant lilacs, mingled with the closer smell of horseflesh. Another farewell party. Already the staples were loaded, the firearms assembled, and wagons renamed for identification: "ILLINOIS TRAIN," "MISSOURI TRAIN," with only one being particularly different: "OREGON OR BUST!" The well-broken oxen were bedded down with the other draft animals in preparation for the long trek ahead.

Rachel could see the scene in her mind's eye—a repeat of the night the few wagons had left the only home she had ever known. The fixed smiles. The hint of tears. The twangy talk of fertile valleys. And a brief, bold flash of gold dust, mingled with a bit of bragging. So the fiddles wailed on and the dancers whirled madly— almost as if the revelers might never see civilization again.

Rachel herself neither felt like joining the festivities nor did she feel like crying over leaving her homeland. Instead, she was examining herself and her marriage— if one could call it that. It was only a marriage of convenience for her. And it was less than that for Cole. How, then, could she account for the slow beat of drums in back of her mind and their quickened tempo when they reached the area of her heart?

She tried to pray. The words seemed to climb only as high as the bows arching like a wooden rainbow across the Conestoga. Her heart kept up its ponderous rhythm; but her spirit, in need of nourishment that only the Lord could provide, melted and then solidified into a lump within her.

Then, above the booming of her heart, there came the sound of muffled voices. Rachel tensed, then relaxed when she realized that the voices were women's. Her relief was short-lived.

"Ain't you heerd? Her pa was a regalar liquor-head. One uv them Scotch-Irish, so it's told to me—keepin' in mind, I don't put no strenth in talebearin' folks."

Mrs. Grant! Rachel's heart slowed and seemed to stop completely. Where or how she had gathered her facts, there was little telling. But one thing was certain: The woman would see to it that the entire wagon train knew—

unless somehow her tongue could be bridled.

For now, Rachel could only hope that the women would move past. She did not feel like coping with anything more tonight. But such was not the case. Unaware that only the wagon sheet separated Rachel from her, Mrs. Grant was telling whoever would listen what she knew of "Cole's peculiar-like marriage."

"Her ma was right purty, so they say—if'n you have a hankerin' fer them that's tall and slim—come from English blood. Fair of face like her daughter but sad of eye. Don't know that she drunk none, tho'—too poorly uv health . . ." The voice tapered off only to resume when one of the group asked a question inaudible to Rachel.

"Oh, prob'ly hated each other, the sad-faced woman and that big, bully of a man. But he had a good eye fer bizness when it come t'that gal uv his'n . . ."

The voices stopped suddenly as footsteps sounded.

"Good evening, ladies." The voice was Cole's. *Oh, praise the Lord!* Rachel was thinking one minute, the next she was wiping at her tears and trying to gain control of herself.

"Rachel?" His rich voice was low and tentative.

Although she was too warm already, Rachel pushed herself further beneath the haven of quilts. Her muffled voice barely audible, she said, "I'm in bed."

"May I come in?"

"I'm in bed, Cole—go away—I—I—"

Then to her absolute horror, she burst into sobs.

Cole was beside her in an instant, his hands holding hers, his face close against her hair in the dark. "What is it, little Rachel? What *is* it?"

Shaken by sobs, Rachel was unable to find a voice. Cole drew her closer and, although she tried to steel herself against the warm stir within, her hands gripped his tighter.

Feeling for her face in the darkness, Cole outlined her nose with a warm finger. "Don't cry, little bunny-face—don't!

Just tell me the trouble so I can fix it." He paused uncertainly. "You can't be—homesick?"

"Oh, Cole, no, *no*! It's just the good-byes and what the others are feeling," she said at last, which was certainly no mistruth. "And how could I be homesick when I so wanted this—this trip—and a new future—a chance at happiness—?"

She stopped short of adding, "With you!"

"Then everything will be all right. Just give me time to prove myself—"

"You've nothing to prove—"

But Cole stopped her in mid-sentence by placing a gentle finger on her lips. "There is one thing I want you to know, Rachel. The morning you saw me coming from the pub—remember?" When she nodded in the darkness, her head bobbing against his chest, Cole continued. "I had an important talk with your father, one that lasted most of the night. I tell you this so you will know you've no more cause to worry. Just accept what I did as a gift and in no way intended to make you feel obligated or embarrassed."

Cole's words were almost a plea. The kind of plea *she* should be making to *him*! It made no sense that he should be apologizing—unless—

"How did you know what my father was up to—I mean, it was not until later that we talked. I don't want you to be placed in the position with the others—those unprincipled men. Oh, Cole, they were so horrible—like gnomes or creatures from a nightmare!" She tried unsuccessfully to effect a laugh.

But Cole's voice when he spoke held no humor.

"I know, dear one, I know. I wish I could undo what has been done to you—" Cole's voice was more wistful than it needed to be. "He and I talked the day you and I became acquainted. He wanted money to satisfy his insatiable need for liquor, so I felt the money was well spent—"

"But he owed you already. He promised to repay you, but you know he won't, don't you?"

"Yes, Rachel, I know. And we need not speak of it again."

Do I imagine it, Rachel wondered, *or does he seem anxious to close the subject?* She felt a deeper sense of respect than before—so deep that she longed to put her arms out to him in gratitude and love. *Oh, why can't he see?*

"Cole," she began softly, "I owe you so much—"

"Don't, Rachel! Please don't say that. You owe me nothing—nothing at all!" The words came out in something akin to harshness. "And now we have a long trip ahead of us so I suggest you get some sleep."

His lips brushed her forehead, lingered a moment, only to push her away almost roughly with a little moan. The moment was broken by a little whine at the back of the wagon.

"Moreover has sniffed me out," Cole said in a normal voice as he backed out between the canvas flaps. It occurred to Rachel that she had not come to know the dog—as she, in many ways, had not come to know her husband.

What is keeping us apart? she asked herself over and over. Cole seemed not to mind in the least the circumstances of the marriage into which she had drawn him. The answer then could lie only in the fact that he was still in love with the girl mentioned by the other women.

Wishing she were older and wiser, Rachel prayed for hours—agonizing at points. "Make me worthy of him, Lord," she begged, "for I know You have sent me the right man." She paid no heed to the passing over of the near-full moon or the darkness that followed—darkness second only to that in her heart.

• • •

Before daybreak the next morning Julius Doogan sounded his bugle long and loud. Rachel, dressing hurriedly in the dark, heard Brother Davey match the bugle's reveille with high-pitched words.

"These'er seasoned travelers, sonny. No doubt up long afore you. So what'er you tryin' to do—shatter the walls of Jericho agin? Enough t'split a body's eardrums!"

The younger man blew a couple of bonus notes. And then there were the hustle-bustle sounds of preparation for departure. Rachel's weariness and apprehensions vanished, giving way to a surge of excitement as she lighted a candle.

"Forgive me, Lord, for not kneeling," she whispered while braiding her hair with shaking fingers. "But You'll be traveling with us and we can talk all the way. Just let me lean on the faith You've given me, remembering always Your promise that faith is the shield of the Christian."

She was securing the braid around her head with a heavy comb when there was a faint, but familiar, whine outside the wagon. "Moreover?" she called into the darkness.

Cautiously, a shadow moved toward her. "Come on, boy—looking for Cole, are you?"

Mention of Cole's name brought the bulky shadow into the little pool of light furnished by the candle.

Rachel withdrew the friendly hand she had extended, for before her stood the most enormous dog she had ever seen. She had expected to see a lanky, spindle-legged animal. Instead, there was a canine monster! Covered with bristly blue-gray hair, the body was long, with well-sprung ribs, and great breadth across the hips which appeared to end without a tail. The head, carried arrogantly high, raised a little higher as if the dog were trying desperately to show his worth.

Rachel continued to stare in astonishment, taking no note that the eyes fastened on her were gentle.

"You're a *dog*?" she finally managed to say. "Cole's dog?"

The animal wagged his hind parts and the missing

tail began wagging. When he would have taken a step closer, Rachel let out a little cry.

At that moment Cole stepped out of the darkness. "It's time you two were meeting."

"I thought you owned a *hound*," Rachel managed.

Cole reached out a hand and the dog eased his great head beneath it, begging to be stroked. Cole patted him gently while answering Rachel. "Irish wolfhound—considered the proper gift for European royalty. But, more importantly, the breed can catch anything that runs! Fiercely loyal—"

Rachel nodded. "Give me time—time to grow accustomed to having him around."

"And me, Rachel?"

Too surprised to reply, Rachel was grateful when another man, a stranger to her, joined them.

"Rachel," Cole said in his usual tone, "I wanted you to meet the wagon master I brought with me, 'Buckeye' Jones. Jones, this is my wife."

Wife! Isn't that the first time Cole used the word? With a throbbing heart, Rachel extended her hand to the wagon master. Something about him was likeable. Tall and dark, he appeared to be a man of brawn born of hard work. His eyes, she saw, had little creases of white which intersected at the corners as if he perpetually squinted against the sun. They were earthtone in color, like his skin—reminding her of the shadows that crept from hiding places to rub out the trail.

And yet there was something about the man that showed an inner hurt and a certain shyness that added to his appeal. "Good to know you, Mrs. Lord," he said shyly. "Cole and I have been friends for many years."

Rachel smiled. "Friends are one of God's most precious gifts," she said, thinking of Aunt Em who would be with her on the journey and Yolanda with whom she would be reunited in Oregon.

The two men's talk flowed around her as Rachel rolled

up her bedding and freshened her face with a splash of water from the granite basin. No time for breakfast, they said . . . just coffee. The wagon master and Cole would ride ahead, with Doogan bringing up the rear. Cattle would present a problem . . .

Rachel realized then that Cole was speaking to her, "I will join you as soon as I can . . ." he promised just as the call "Spre-e-e-ad out!" came and one by one the wagons lurched forward.

17

Growing Accustomed to the Trail

Aunt Em joined Rachel in "Cole's Wagon Number One." The two women did not talk much. Rachel was buried in her own thoughts. Aunt Em seemed to be, too. In spite of the planning, there seemed to be more confusion here than there had been on the day of departure from her hometown. The wagons had traveled only a few miles out on the rolling prairies before sunset. The new cattle which had joined the caravan had to learn what the more experienced cows knew already—that they were not to wander in search of grass. There was muttering among those who owned no cattle, causing Agnes Grant to move from wagon to wagon—wearing a doomsday expression and announcing, "There's trouble ahead fer certain!"

When "Buckeye" rode back to tell of a small stream ahead, there was a sigh of relief from the travelers. Only one day out and already trouble seemed to be brewing. "Mutterin' like the children of Israel—and with nary a cause." Aunt Em shook her head with a look of despair. "Now me'n my Davey brought nothin' into this world and don't figger on takin' anythin' out. But we plan on *leavin'* a lot to folks with willin' ears." She chuckled. "Don't even own ourselves a wagon; but the Lord provided when He learned we was wantin' to go to Oregon!"

In a rush of gratitude, Rachel burst out, "He provided for me, too—a way *up*, like you said, if not a way *out*—"

"You'll not be wantin' a way out with Cole, dearie."

Rachel was silent, but there was within her a growing conviction that Emmaline Galloway—who possessed God's gift of an understanding heart—was keenly aware that there were some things Rachel did not wish to explain. Neither would she be asking. Rachel longed to confide, but where more than here did the Golden Rule apply? Would she want Cole explaining their strange circumstances? "God forbid," she whispered.

Silence reigned again. And again it was Aunt Em who broke it. "There it is!" She pointed with pleasure toward the tired-looking little stream that dug its way sluggishly through the prairie floor. "Whoa back, Napoleon. Think you're a match fer Hannibal?" she asked the mule concerning Cole's black stallion.

The wagon slowed as Aunt Em slackened the reins. "Here!" she said suddenly, handing the reins to Rachel. "You'll be drivin' some of the time. Might as well get used to the feel. *Gee* means right. *Haw* means left. And you gotta put meanin' in your voice. No critter pays a mind to a weak leader."

As the reins changed hands, the mules turned slightly. "Tighten up a smitherin'," Aunt Em advised. "Not too much now—"

Rachel followed directions with a growing sense of confidence. One mule snorted. Then, ears drooping, the team relaxed. Rachel felt a thrill of pleasure and was ready to express appreciation to Aunt Em for rushing her into a lesson in driving. Before there was time, Aunt Em spoke.

"Can you ride?"

"Yes, I ride well."

Aunt Em climbed stiffly from the wagon. "That's good," she said, extending a rough hand to Rachel. "And now let's get to learnin' camp cookin'. Wanna wash up first?"

Rachel nodded, wondering where the other woman found strength to start unloading the heavy dinner pot, enormous black skillet, and granite utensils. She herself could scarcely move. Her body was one giant ache, beginning along her spine and following to all the nerve endings. Stiffly, she forced one foot ahead of the other, limping painfully toward the murky stream.

There were several wagons to pass—each, she noticed, piled high with the only possessions the emigrants had salvaged from their former homes. Quick glimpses revealed trunks and dressers wedged between packing barrels and sacks of grain. In one she saw small seedling trees—fruit trees, undoubtedly.

At least, there would be lumber in the new land—loads of it, according to Yolanda's letters. Rachel recalled one letter in particular:

> This settlement is not a place of man's creation—not even of white man's naming. It would be a beautiful townsite—a round hill some ten miles in circumference, the north side covered with fir timber, oak, hazel, and various kinds of underwood. But who could be so heartless as to hack away the haven for deer, bear, wolves, and elk? Anyway, the timber's considered worthless with no way of hauling it away. But

there will come a day, I am sure, when the mixed blessings of civilization will come; for the soil is rich, black, deep, and fertile. Our settlement slopes to what looks like the River of Life, fed as it is by the rain-swollen streamlets that spend their lives just satisfying its thirst...so pure...so crystal clear...baptizing the valley with love...

Remembering that letter, Rachel bent over stiffly above the sluggish stream at the campsite. It took a great deal of courage to scoop up the yellowish liquid and splash it on her sunburned face. When she rose and faced the direction from which the last breeze had come, she did not feel refreshed. For a moment, she fanned herself with the palm of her hand. Then, feeling her face tighten, she reached to touch it with experimental fingers, only to cry out in horror. For her face was covered with a mask of silt. Frantically grabbing the hem of her skirt, she wiped at the caked mud, only to realize that the skin beneath it was dry and—in her distressed state of mind—withered, ugly, and old.

A tear slid down her face and then another—each taking with it a measure of the scum and splashing into spots of discoloration onto her exposed petticoats. Seeing the damage, Rachel was unable to let go of her calico skirt. Instead, she knotted it with both hands—overcome by a desperation she did not understand herself.

But Cole did! When a strong pair of masculine arms closed about her, Rachel did not struggle. Neither was it necessary for her to look up to know in whose gentle embrace she stood. She had no right to be here. Everything between them was in limbo...and she looked like a mud pie! But none of this mattered, none of it at all. It was enough to be held close to the muscular body and feel the circle of protection of her husband's arms. It did not occur to her to resist.

When she could speak, she said brokenly, "Oh, Cole, I wanted to be a good wife, at least, a companion—"

"Who says you aren't?" Cole was busy wiping her face with an enormous red bandanna.

"Oh, Cole! Why did you marry me? I—"

"Hold still, will you? I married you for your beauty, of course—so now let me get you cleaned up so I can see that face again!"

Say more, Cole. Please say more. But when he spoke again, it was the experienced man who had made the trip over the Oregon Trail—at least, partway—before. And one of those times he had a woman with him. That memory must be standing between them—so different for him than this meaningless marriage. Shame flowed over her anew.

Chilled by the haunting memories of Templeton Buchanan's vulgar exploitation of her, Rachel was warmed by Cole's sudden smile. Mentally chiding herself for her lack of control and grace, she tried to smile back as she listened.

"It will be easier as you grow accustomed to the trail. That I promise. And I will be on hand to help. I hope you will remember that—and trust me, Rachel. We have to build on that trust."

Trust? Why did everyone keep using that word? It hung between the two of them invisibly, scarring any possible understanding they could reach. *Trust Cole?* There was no reason for her to do otherwise.

Realizing Cole's eyes were still on her, Rachel nodded. "Of course I trust you, Cole. I trust you implicitly, but—"

His brow lifted in wonder. "I thank the Lord for that—and now before the others come looking for us, we should get back." Taking her elbow, he steered her past the long line of oxen, mules, cows, and a few horses which were hurrying to the stream, bellowing and nickering in thirst.

"The water's for the livestock. At least, until we run low. It's all right for you to use what you need from the wagons. Unlike your face, we can replace it!"

Feeling better, Rachel laughed. "You mean I won't always have to look like this?"

"You're beautiful any way you are, my dear, sweet Rachel." His eyes moved appreciatively over the mud-streaked fragility of her features, glowing with the kind of warmth she so longed for.

Brother Davey, his graying beard bristling from the sides of his face and drooping from below his chin, was busily driving pegs for the night quarters. Rachel wondered, as she hurried past, how the four of them would manage in a single tent. Then, seeing Aunt Em bustling about a camp-fire, she ducked into the wagon to tidy up before joining her.

"Come see how a hoecake's done," Aunt Em called out as Rachel approached. "Got the idee from the Indians when we was in Oklahoma Territory a spell. Batter's cornmeal and buttermilk. Bring the buttermilk, Davey!"

Muttering, her husband dropped the mallet and hurried away, leaving Rachel to wonder where on earth he would find buttermilk. Before she could ask, Aunt Em explained.

"The mornin' milk's put in barrels and churns itself as the wagons bump along. So there'll be butter for this hoe-cake. Used to bake 'em on a hoe down South—sorta simplifies pullin' 'em from a pan. But, then, this'll be a heap tastier, hungry as we are."

Brother Davey, still muttering, handed a crock of butter-milk to his wife, who ignored his muttering and went on talking to Rachel. "See, jest dump the whole thing in the buttered skillet, flip it like a flapjack, and there you are!" she said, triumphantly turning out the enor-mous, crusty cake onto a tin pan. "Got the potatoes peeled, Davey?"

The meal was delicious. Aunt Em, who had hidden a few eggs in her apron pocket, knew exactly how an egg should be fried. The bacon was lean and crisp, and the hoecake was rich and buttery. The coffee was even "strong enough to walk," to quote Brother Davey. As the four of them sat cross-legged around their little fire, it was as if the rest of the world were shut out. Rachel, raising her eyes to the star-strewn dome above them, wished the moment might go on forever. She was learning a new kind of togetherness.

When Brother Davey raised his voice in a long, wordy prayer after the meal, Rachel lowered her head in a silent prayer all her own. It seemed only normal that Cole's long fingers would close over hers. Following his example, she reached and clasped Aunt Em's. Aunt Em's reaching to take her husband's hand surprised the man so much, he became flustered, his voice faltering as he joined hands with Cole to complete the circle.

"So, Lord, we thank You for all this bounty—seein' it was You who created the land and the water underneath the firmament . . . and it was You, then, who divided the men from the women . . ."

"The light from the darkness!" Aunt Em corrected.

"That, too!" Brother Davey affirmed. "So ended the morning and the evening of the first day. Amen!"

18

Estrellita

A pattern established the first night was to last for awhile at least. Cole, speaking in low tones to Brother Davey, explained that Mr. Doogan and the wagon master must have their proper rest. Would Brother Davey be willing to stand watch with him? Cole asked.

"Yes, yes, of course! Jest let them Injuns come anywheres near here...and the same applies to the looters...and, as fer wild animals—well, now, I'll see to it that the lamb and the lion lay down together—elsewise one is apt to end up in the dinner pot and t'other

I'll skin alive to teach th' other lions a lesson!"

Rachel, her head resting on drawn-up knees beside the dying embers of the campfire, could imagine Brother Davey's stance went along with his tone of importance. Drawn up to his full height, he was still a head shorter than Aunt Em, but Cole's invitation probably drew him up on tiptoe.

The image made her smile. But Cole's response, obviously not intended for her ears, was guarded. "I'm more concerned about loss of livestock at this point. And there's to be no shooting, as you know, except for the protection of life. A single shot can bring Indians from out of nowhere. Otherwise, they're apt to let us pass in peace."

"Maybe hereabouts," Brother Davey was mumbling. "More hostile down the way apiece." Cole was unruffled. A day at a time, he advised...no panic...and then Rachel heard him say distinctly, "Keep a special eye on my other wagon. You know how precious the cargo is..."

Cole's voice drifted away in the hushed stillness. When she lifted her head, he was gone, leaving her to ponder the meaning of his words about the other wagon's cargo.

The raucous laughter and snatches of song which had filled the night air were silent. Only the *scrape-scrape* of the hoe Aunt Em was dragging through the ashes to make sure no live coals remained broke the quiet.

"Means we'll be occupyin' th' tent, dearie," the older woman said, picking up threads of the men's conversation. Then with practicality she began restacking pots and pans. Rachel rose wordlessly to help.

"Aunt Em," she said, as casually as she could manage, "what do you plan on doing in Oregon—farming?"

"Why, I dunno." Emmaline Galloway's voice was noncommittal, almost unconcerned. "My Davey's thinkin' some on circuit ridin'. The missionaries done a fair job in the beginnin'...but," she sighed, "like my old ma used t'say, 'A new broom sweeps clean.' But seems t'me the rest of us best snatch at the crumbs they piled up and carry on the Lord's work. There'll be work fer all— 'specially us women, standin' by our men. If you gotta question, come right out with it, Rachel!"

Caught off guard, Rachel bit her lip. She was tempted to deny that anything bothered her. But, struggling with the partial conversation she had overheard, she asked a question to which Aunt Em might presume she knew the answer.

"Has Cole shared his plans with you?"

"You mean about—wait a minute! Has he shared 'em with *you*?"

"No." The single word was a pained whisper.

"Like I said, you gotta question, come right out 'n ask it, Rachel." Aunt Em's arms, large and comforting were around her. "Maybe that would start fixin' the wrongs that need a-rightin' between my two fav'rit children."

So Aunt Em knew. And Agnes Grant knew. And what one woman would guard with her life, the other would cast about like pearls before the swine. The disturbing thought gnawed at the fragile shell of protection she had built up around her long after her prayers were over.

After a hurried breakfast the next morning, the wagon master, who most of the travelers called Buck, came to announce to Cole that the party would be crossing into Kansas soon.

Rachel sensed disquiet in Cole's question. "Expect problems with the Indians?"

"No." Buck's voice was quiet like his eyes and his manner in general. "Most of them have taken to farming since our last attempt to get through."

"And the Kansas River?"

"We'll be all right if the weather holds. Thought I should give you a count of people in the party, Cole. There are 895 of us, 265 being men—counting all boys over 16 as men— and only 130 women. The rest are children."

Rachel remembered the long line of wagons she had watched crawl over the dusty roads during one of her walks. Aunt Em had insisted on "leg stretchin' " on the hour. The walk did her body a world of good and Rachel was happy to meet some of the other women and chat. Too, she had felt a strange sense of pride in the caravan of adventurous people of which she was a small part and her husband, obviously, was so great a part. Everyone, she noted, spoke of Mr. Lord with respect.

But now she felt apprehensive at Buck Jones' report. She shuddered inwardly at the thought of 265 men, most of them boys, trying to stall off an Indian attack. The Kansas Indians were not hostile, Buck said, so she could relax. But some inner sense caused her to look over her shoulder at a passing shadow. And suddenly her gaze was locked with that of Julius Doogan. She did not like what she saw in that fleeting glance as he slouched toward the rear of the wagon train. Her woman's intuition told her that here was a man of indelicate scruples. *Brother Davey's hunch about him has been right all along—or am I being too judgmental?* All the same, she deemed it unwise to wander far enough back to encounter the skulking young man in her frequent walks.

The days took on a sameness. Rachel would hardly have known one day from the other except for notations she made in *Poor Richard's Almanac*, which she had salvaged from her mother's few belongings. Maybe the book with all its advice on planting and harvesting would be helpful in the garden she hoped to have in Oregon. She and Cole would build a cabin, twine morning glories around the door—and she wondered how many children he wanted? Then she would pull herself from the momentary reverie and quickly banish the thought. Only to have it recur when another night's darkness closed down—without Cole. So the nights took on a sameness, too.

Then they were in the area of the Siouan tribes on the

lower Kansas River where the men decided crossing might be easier. A swarthy-faced man, wearing an ancient felt hat over his long braids, met the train and lifted a peaceful hand. "Praise the Lord," Aunt Em whispered. Rachel, whose heart was a rock in her throat, could only nod.

"Kaw," the man said, pointing up and down the river, then making a wide arc with his welcoming hand. "Kaw, name for big water, big land—big *man*!"

Cole strode toward him, spoke something in a tongue Rachel did not understand, pointing to the water and then back to the wagon train. The old Indian appeared to consider, then pointed to a steep incline, raised his hands and mumbled as if chanting a prayer.

Cole left the man, who stood expressionless and cross-armed, and returned to report that *kaw* meant the whole of Kansas: a section of the Siouan tribes, the river, and the land. The tribesman would help, providing he could come by some alcohol for his people who had "the shakes."

Julius Doogan spoke up immediately, "Give the old buzzard whatever he wants—"

Cole's powerful jaw tightened. "That'll do, Doogan." His voice was firm, final. "There will be no alcohol distributed to the Indians. And I suggest that you refrain from using such words in regard to these people. It is their territory through which we're passing. We need their help."

Doogan's eyes shifted nervously from one person to another, pausing to roam Rachel's figure. Praying that Cole did not see, Rachel quickly averted her eyes and concentrated on what he was saying.

"The river's too deep here, the leader tells me. But if we will come to the hills up there," Cole paused as if wondering how to break the news, then resumed, "he and some of his bucks will help us lower the wagons to where the waters are more shallow."

A cry of alarm went up from the group standing nearby and traveled the length of the 100 wagons.

"There's gonna be trouble." Agnes Grant, who had a talent for covering ground quickly when it came to spreading alarm, muttered darkly to all. "Women folks sayin' they ain't gonna throw 'way furniture...men folks sayin' we need new leadership—"

"Shut up, Aggie!" Aunt Em's voice carried a command. "The main trouble we got in this situation's your tongue! Me and Rachel here'll go back and calm 'em."

Despite her own fears, Rachel felt a surge of something akin to joy that the older woman included her in the job at hand. That she could soothe away the anxieties of another had never occurred to her. But then, she had never thought she could drive a team of horses either!

Quickly, she stepped to Cole's side. "Give me a word of reassurance I can pass along to the other women and I'll help."

Cole looked at her with surprise and appreciation. "Thank you, Rachel," he said gently. Then matter-of-factly he explained that the canyon walls were not very steep and that the stream they would be crossing would be only a small tributary to the Kansas River. He appeared about to say more when, squeezing her hand, he walked hurriedly to join Buck.

Mandy Burnside and Liz Farnall, women Rachel had become acquainted with earlier, helped spread enough words of cheer to rub out the damage done by Agnes Grant. But, beneath the satisfaction of her mission, Rachel felt a certain anxiety twisting beneath the surface. People like Agnes Grant did not take a put-down well. The woman would retaliate. And some inner sense said her vindication would be taken out on Rachel herself instead of Aunt Em. She had enough ammunition already, considering her mischief-making ways. Rachel considered taking Cole into her confidence, but decided against it— he had enough on his mind. She could not talk with Aunt Em without revealing how Cole had come to marry her. Well, she had the Lord above anyway.

One of the men gave a two-fingered whistle, signaling that the wagons were to move on. The women hurried back to their places and soon the teams were straining in their harness to pull the heavy loads up the short, but steep, incline.

Rachel was never sure if she correctly remembered the rest of the ordeal. Later she was to be grateful for the experience she gained for it was only the first of many times she would be assisting with unhitching teams, letting wagons down by means of ropes, and rehitching so they would pull the wagons up the opposite banks. How they accomplished this was, she decided, simply another of God's miracles.

Really, the Lord deserves a time all His own—where people kneel together and pray in thanksgiving. But the time was not right. Many of the travelers would be offended. Others would point out logically that the job was not finished yet—which was true. Mules and oxen were still straining up the slippery banks.

Rachel was aware suddenly of a small tug at her skirt. She glanced down to meet a pair of dark eyes, turned upward questioningly, only to return to the scene below. Other children would be screaming or they would be too busy playing tag to notice. But this one was different. Her eyes were great burning lamps betraying only light, no emotion.

And yet, her small voice whispered fear. "Will they drown, senora—all the men?"

Rachel believed all the strength in her bones had been drained away in the long trek among the wagons. But here was someone who needed her as she had needed another when the world collapsed around her with her mother's death—hurt, angry, confused—and nobody to whom she could turn. It was only a simple question the child asked; but something in the small brown waif's manner said more. Reaching out, Rachel gathered her close—clinging to her as she had once clung to Mother, the only person she had ever loved besides Cole. At least she could comfort.

"Of course, it will be all right, darling." Then, dropping on her knees, she whispered, "Where are your parents?"

The little girl pushed the long silky, black hair from her face and looked away. Holding onto this fragile little being was like trying to clasp a handful of smoke. Something cautioned Rachel to be still.

At length the child spoke. "Me llamo Estrellita."

Feeling that the child would vanish in thin air at any moment, Rachel knelt by her side, struggling with a brief Spanish phrase: "No comprendo espanol."

Hopefully, the great, soulful eyes sought Rachel's, her lips moving rapidly in high-speed Spanish. Rachel could only shake her head. Hope died. The melancholy eyes looked down.

The child seemed a million miles away. And then she turned back to Rachel. "My name is Estrellita. It means Little Star."

"What a lovely name. May I call you Star?"

"You may," she said with a certain sweetness and grace that Rachel had never seen before in so small a child.

"And now, Star, we must let Mother and Daddy know you are safe," Rachel said, rising to her feet and taking hold of the small, brown hand.

Star did not move. Instead, she crouched like a frightened animal—the great eyes now pleading.

"You love me please. You have enough to go 'round?"

Tears rushed to Rachel's eyes. "Oh, darling, of course I love you . . . and I have plenty of love in my heart. But, first, I must find where you belong—"

"To you."

Rachel felt as if some pit had opened before her. Perilously balanced on the rim, she was about to fall in. Too much had happened too fast. And now this.

Gripping the small hand as if it alone could save her from

the black pit below, Rachel whispered, "No parents?"

"Mi madre—" she began, then switched to carefully-rehearsed English. "My mommy died. My father runned. I hid here."

19

♥

Wild River!

Aunt Em, whose heart was sized proportionately with her flesh-endowed body, found in it a special chamber for little Star immediately. "Would you take a likin' to a Joseph's-coat dress?" she asked the child.

Star didn't know. As Rachel drove, Aunt Em dug into her box of quilt scraps. Star's eyes brightened at sight of the bright colors. "But isn't that a boy's name?" Star asked.

Aunt Em caught Rachel's eye and winked. Then, slipping a thimble on her finger, she began cutting and whipping

together the little scraps. As she worked, she told Star
a story as brilliant as the pieces she joined together about
a little boy who had a coat of many colors who was
stolen away...only to become a king who could help his
people.

Star sat between the two women, her tiny body carefully
erect, her face expressionless. But when the story was finished, she whispered, "Yes, I would take a likin' to a
Joseph's-coat dress."

Then the small head drooped onto Rachel's shoulder and
she was fast asleep.

A sharp bend in the trail brought the wagon train
to the Kansas River again. The murmurings were worse
than before. "We've crossed a'ready...we've lost the
trail...our cattle'll drown, which is most likely th' whole
idee!"

Calming the travelers would be more difficult this time,
Rachel realized with a sick heart as she gazed upon the roil-
ing river swollen with flood waters. Cole would need her
support. So thinking, she was at his side before the last
wagon had stopped.

Tall and straight as an archer's arrow, Cole stood with
his back to her studying the course of the water. She
wondered if his shoulders ever grew tired of the load he
was bearing for all these people—most of them ungrateful.
There was an air of isolation about him, something that
made her long to reach out and smooth the tired lines away.
Feeling her presence, Cole turned.

"Rachel!" he said with genuine pleasure. "I'm glad you've
come." And taking her left hand, he tucked it beneath his
arm. "We've a real problem—and I'm not sure where help's
to come from."

"As the Good Book says, 'Look to the hills...' Oh, *Cole*,
LOOK!"

To the right, the terrain rose a bit and over the rapids
an elfin man was manning a wide boat and waving a fran-
tic welcome. "Oho, there, pardner! Thees boat's she's a

ferry!" his voice rang out over the slap of the unpeeled poles he used for oars.

"An answer to an unspoken prayer! Maybe we can make it after all."

"Of course, we can make it! Just as I told little Star we would."

"Little who?" But Cole was busily signaling to the man below and she doubted if he heard her brief explanation.

"I'll spread the word, Cole." Rachel turned to go.

"You're a wonder, Rachel—you really are."

"I know," she said playfully, for in spite of the seriousness of all that faced them, she felt a certain elation. Cole needed her. Star needed her. So did these people. So that meant that God needed her, too!

Before Rachel got as far as "Cole's Wagon Number One," she saw Brother Davey coming in a dead run. He was too out of breath to talk, a situation so rare that Rachel had a chance to explain. But all the while he was wagging his head.

When at last he could manage words, he gasped, "Git back to thet snappin' turtle named Aggie. She and him . . . thet whippersnapper Doogan's cookin' up no good . . ."

Rachel waited to hear no more. She rushed forward, calling over her shoulder for Star to stick close to Aunt Em. Hardly aware of what she said, Rachel promised the others that help had come as she hurried on toward the rear wagon.

"Why, Miz Lord, whatever can you be doin' so fer from that young husband now?" Agnes Grant's mocking voice stopped Rachel in her tracks. "I was just enjoyin' the time uv day with our capable campin' aide here—"

Julius Doogan, who had been walking with Mrs. Grant, gave Rachel a knowing look and stopped close beside her. "My, my, I wish I'd known you were up for grabs," he whispered, allowing his heavy-lidded eyes to travel her length in an insulting way before breaking into a run to reach the river.

The humiliation and shame were back, but Rachel tried to bridle the anger in her voice. "What have you told him?" she asked the older woman tonelessly.

"Why nothin' that ain't common knowledge—"

"*What?*"

"That Colby Lord bought hisself a wife—"

Something inside Rachel ignited and burst into flame. "That's not true. And you'd better pass the word to Julius Doogan before Cole hears of it. Now, get out of my sight!"

The woman cringed before Rachel's rage. Then, like a sparrow hawk determined to get its prey, she called over her shoulder as she fled, "Ain't no lie—and you're gonna cause trouble!"

For a moment, Rachel stood still, biting her lip until it throbbed like her pulse, scarcely aware that other travelers were rushing past. Then the moment was gone. Angry voices had risen from the direction of the river. She was needed.

Even as she ran, one man's voice rose above the others to reach her ears while she was yet a distance away. "Why, of all th' dirty connivin'! Them two pairin' up t'charge a king's ransom fer crossin' a river on that rat trap. How much *you* rakin' off from the Frenchman, Lord?"

"Yeah, must be Colby Lord's idee. Plain t'see that furriner ain't got the brains to figger on takin' helpless people in."

And suddenly everything was out of control. No amount of reasoning was going to do any good. One group of men began hammering and sawing some pieces of timber for making their own raft. When Cole tried to reason with the group, a burly arm shot from somewhere in the crowd to graze the leader's chin. With a little cry, Rachel tried to reach him. But the angry mob would not part to let her pass. She lost sight of him completely. She saw neither Buck nor Brother Davey.

And Star! Where was she? Rachel managed to ease her slender body through the crowd and run back in the general direction of Cole's wagons, whispering a prayer.

There was no sign of Aunt Em. And then Rachel heard the other woman's voice above the bedlam by the river-bank. "Star . . . Star . . . Estrel-li-ta!" Calling. Calling. But there was no answer. It was as if the fairylike creature had returned to the vapor from which she was made.

Panic such as she had never known before welled up in Rachel's throat. Tormenting visions flashed before her eyes: Star flailing thin little arms and legs in the murky river; Star swept downstream leaving only a little whirlpool where the tiny body had been; Star, feeling unloved, running away . . .

Others joined in the search outside. Rachel was tempted to run to the river, but something clicked in her mind. The child had loved the wagon, found comfort there, and gone to sleep to the rocking rhythm of the turning wheels.

She ran to the back of the wagon, opened the flaps with a pounding heart, and waited until her eyes adjusted to the semidarkness. There was no sign of life, but something told Rachel the child was there. Noiselessly, she crawled into the wagon and began searching with her heart as well as with her eyes. *Be here, darling, be here . . .*

It was a strange whine that alerted her. "Moreover?" Rachel whispered, crawling cautiously toward the sound. And there in the corner, bunched in a little lump of sleep— one nut-brown hand on the dog's head, the other clutching her Joseph's-coat dress to her heart—lay little Star.

Overcome with joy, Rachel reached out her arms and gathered both dog and child to her. Star clung to her even before she was fully awake.

"Oh, darling," Rachel whispered, realizing then how much this lost child had come to mean in so short a time, "you scared me half to death. Why were you here?"

Star, trying to rub sleep from her enormous eyes, said solemnly, "I was waiting for my mommy."

When the full impact of the words dawned on Rachel, she held little Star even closer—feeling some inner desire fulfilled, one she had never known she possessed. Estrellita who had come to her out of God's Mysterious Nowhere was no longer a child of vapor. She was real—a flesh and blood child, hers to love, to have, and to hold. Hers to cherish. Oh, she couldn't wait to tell Cole!

Rachel, holding Star's hand with Moreover wagging closely behind, reached the riverbank just in time to see a horrifying scene—one so multi-faceted she was unable to take it all in at a single glance.

The flimsy raft built by men who objected to the Frenchman's charge, had been placed on two canoes and loaded with household goods. Rachel watched with pounding heart as the men began propelling the makeshift craft toward the opposite shore. The Frenchman had overloaded his "ferry" with women, children, and their personal belongings. Even as he pushed off with the pole for an oar, it was obvious that one corner was under water.

Cattle and horses were attempting to swim across the wild river.

"Will they drown—the people and the animals?"

Little Star's question brought Rachel back to the world around her. So she reassured the child as she had before. "Of course not, darling. Do you know how to pray?"

Star nodded solemnly and made a cross on her heart... just as the Frenchman's boat went under! There were screams from the women and children, oaths from the men... and then Rachel saw Cole, Brother Davey, and Buck Jones plunge into the water.

All Rachel could remember was her fervent praying until she felt the fleshy comfort of Aunt Em's arms about her.

"They've hauled 'em ashore. My Davey could whip a bear with a switch, he could!"

20

"Tell Me About Our Daughter!"

"I wonder if I could have the honor of your company on a bit of a stroll this evening—and find out just how we came to have a daughter!"

Cole's question, so lightly asked after the crises-filled days, caught Rachel by surprise. She had longed to talk with him about Star's sudden appearance, ask his advice—and praise him highly for bringing the restless travelers back into some semblance of order. But there were so many demands on his time that the young wife felt she should add no more.

Now Cole's words undid her completely. The walk with him she would welcome. But his reference to their having a daughter unleashed a new emotion, one that was both wild and sweet—but somehow, strangely sad. Unexpected tears trembled on her eyelashes and Rachel turned away quickly to hide them.

"You mean you didn't hear?" Rachel said falteringly, remembering her attempt to alert him.

"I heard only a rumor," Cole teased. "But I don't recall you knitting little garments—"

"Oh, Colby Lord, stop it!" she commanded sternly. Then they both burst into the kind of laughter that comes when a too-tight spring is released.

The night was black and starry-eyed. Rachel was glad there was no moon. *Talking will be easier this way*, she thought, as they strolled away from the wagons. Finding a little knoll, they sat down side by side in the intimate dark.

Somewhere in the distance there was the hungry cry of a wolf. When Rachel shivered, Cole placed a warm, protective arm about her shoulders.

"About Star?" he asked gently.

Rachel told him the strange story then and together they puzzled over it. "But, oh, Cole, you'll love her!" Rachel promised.

"We've met," Cole answered, much to Rachel's surprise. "It was inevitable," he chuckled, "seeing that she and Moreover are inseparable."

Of course. Rachel smiled in the darkness. "Then she can stay?"

"Stay? Just what do you think we would do with a little piece of lost humanity out here otherwise, my dear Mrs. Lord?"

My dear Mrs. Lord! Rachel's heart began to beat erratically, but she tried to keep her voice casual. "I mean, Cole, that we have never really spoken of—well, finances, the food supply—and you already have one extra mouth to feed."

"A man's wife is not 'a mouth to feed,' " he said huskily, his arm tightening slightly about her. "And if that wife happens to acquire a daughter, that goes for her, too!"

"Oh, Cole—" Tears coursed down her face unashamedly. "You are so wonderful—so strong, so caring, so *invincible*—"

Cole interrupted her words by placing a warm hand gently over her mouth. Something told her he did not trust himself to speak. Then, dropping his hand suddenly, he rose.

"I don't deserve those words, Rachel. Someday you will know that and, in the knowing, will come to hate me."

"Never!" she cried out in alarm as she sprang from where she sat and, with one forward motion, was in his arms.

The touch of his hand was almost unbearably gentle as he traced the outline of her face. "I will lose you, little bunny-face. I will lose you and I can't bear it."

"Is it—was it the other girl?" she whispered from where her face was buried against the corded strength of his chest. "Aunt Em has told me a little—how much you've been through, conquered, learned to live with, and grown stronger because of it. Tell me about her, Cole—"

"It isn't the way you think, Rachel. And I beg you to give me time—just a little time. I have every intention of baring my soul to you. And you own my heart already."

"Then what—" Rachel began then stopped short of adding "is holding us apart?" Time. Cole had asked for time. She had no right to push him into a relationship which, for some reason, he was unprepared. And how could she, who had always been so restrained, be so daring—so, so *unladylike*!

Because I'm in love, that's how. I'm a new person—a WHOLE person. You know that, Lord, and—knowing that—You will understand that I am no more able to part with Cole than with the child You have sent to me. Her lips were silent. But her heart cried out to the starry sky.

And then her breath quickened, her cheeks as warm as the sultry breeze that blew off the river. How, oh *how*, could she have forgotten her promise to give Cole his freedom at the end of the trail? And here she was telling God she was unable to.

Rachel realized suddenly that Cole was talking. "—and her only responses to me so far are in her native tongue. It probably gives her a measure of security—like the wagon where she hid."

"Do you have any idea where Star came from? She speaks English very well—with me. Her mother is dead. Her father deserted her. Maybe that accounts for her shyness with men."

"Probably does," Cole said slowly. "As to where she came from, I've a feeling she's from one of the trains which were attacked and most massacred. Undoubtedly, she's still in shock. All the more reason to love her. And there's plenty of food, Rachel. I thought you knew I was financing most of this trip."

No, she hadn't known. Yet knowing made her love him all the more. Rachel reached out and took his hand as they left the little knoll.

21

Across Blue River

April turned to May—a time for wild flowers and songbirds. A time for love. But the section of country the train was passing through had turned into scrub desert beaten raw by wind and sun. If those were mountains beyond the shimmer of heat waves, they were too far-distant for birds to fly to these wastelands for a serenade. And, as for love, one could only feel it in the heart. Every word, every wakening thought, was directed toward survival.

But Rachel had grown used to the routine of driving,

stretching her legs when it was Aunt Em's turn, helping pitch camp, and preparing a meal over an open fire. She and Star made a game of looking for buffalo chips and mesquite wood for the fire—a game which Moreover looked forward to, his nose to the ground in search of an animal trail.

"I'm teaching 'el perro' the names of animals in Spanish," Star volunteered on one of their evening hunts.

Seizing the opportunity to speak of the child's past, Rachel said, "It is good that you speak two languages, darling. How did you learn so much so young?"

The tiny figure with the great, dark eyes looked up, her own gaze as questioning as Rachel's. It was almost as if she were questioning Rachel. Almost, yes, as if there had been no previous life—and Rachel found herself at times believing it. Surely God must have sent her this fragile creature with a will of iron—an endurance, an instinct for survival, and a gift of loving other children did not seem to possess. Rachel knew then that the child would forever be a mystery. Nobody was coming for her. And, bewilderingly, little Star had accepted her new mother—and even Cole as father—without question.

"How old *are* you, Star?"

Rachel, her eyes bright with unshed tears, looked deeply into the small, brown face so far below her own. Then, for the first time, the great eyes brightened and the corners of Star's mouth lifted in a hint of a smile. In response to the question, she held up four brown fingers which she immediately made into a baby fist just right for grasping the ruff on Moreover's neck. Then, with a distinct little "We love you!" child and dog skipped into the private world whose boundaries adults can never cross again.

• • •

For several days travel was relatively easy. The ground was flat and the wagons made good time. Discontented murmurs had died to whispers. Rachel, having gleaned nothing more from Yolanda's letters than that the trip was long but worthwhile when one reached the promised glory of Oregon, hoped that the worst was over.

"Aggie's still spreadin' tales, but nobody's payin' much attention best I can tell," Aunt Em commented once.

That was almost too good to be true, but Rachel was only too happy to believe it. Sometime it would have to be dealt with undoubtedly; but Cole would handle it. All he asked was her trust—and he certainly had that.

The only other problem was Julius Doogan. What might he say? And yes, what might he do? Following a woman's instinct, Rachel steered clear of him completely. If there was a problem, she looked for Cole. But he rode so far in advance of the train that she saw him far less than she would have liked, so she sought Brother Davey or Buck.

Buck, she had discovered, was a much deeper person than she had believed at first. He was always ready to listen, his head cocked to one side, eyes squinting in concentration. And always understanding in the way a human being who has been hurt by life recognizes hurt in another. Yes, Cole was fortunate to have him as wagon master—even more fortunate to have him as a friend.

And then it was June, June 6th to be exact, Rachel noted in her almanac. The day began as all others: early breakfast and the long train far down the dusty trail before the pink of sunrise. The train moved along at a good clip—only to come to a sudden halt.

"Blue River crossing!" The cry began at the head of the wagon train and echoed down the long procession.

"No Frenchman's comin' t' th' rescue 'way out here," Brother Davey said, yanking at his side-whiskers in concentration. "So what do you propose, boys?"

He directed the question to Cole and Buck, pointedly ignoring Julius Doogan. But it was he who responded anyway.

"Why not wade across on our knees so we can be praying

all the while? I'm surprised *you* didn't think of that!" His chuckle was unpleasant.

The minister's eyes darkened like angry thunderclouds as he took a step toward the man who had taunted him. "Say what you will t' me. But I ain't gonna have you insultin' th' Almighty!"

Cole walked between the two men. From behind the wagon where Rachel watched uneasily, it was plain to see that Cole, too, was angry. His words, though controlled, carried a hint of contempt.

"I should let him at you, Doogan. You've asked for it since the beginning. Now, my advice to you—"

"My advice to *you* is to mind your own business—and the way I hear it, you have plenty!"

Cole's face darkened and his broad jaw tightened. "I've a hunch there's a hidden meaning to those words. And I suggest you *keep* it hidden until our day of reckoning. Subject closed! Now," he said calmly, "there's work to do." And with the sense of conviction that was so much a part of him, Cole outlined a plan whereby the wagon beds could be propped up and the river forded. And, Rachel—masking her inner turmoil with calmness matching her husband's—hurried back to prepare the women.

Star clung tightly to Rachel's hand as Cole waded out to test the depth of the river's west fork. Her dusky eyes wore the expression of a child who has been swung too high. But she did not scream out like the other children did as their fathers moved into the water. And this time it was she who spoke words of comfort to Rachel.

"He will not drown—my father."

Rachel picked the child up and held her close. Unable to trust her voice, she nodded. But she could not stop crying. *Oh, Lord,* her heart whispered silently as she watched Cole's every move, *guide us into giving little Star the love that every child should have.*

She realized then that she had been praying as a parent—

and as Cole's wife! Without dealing with the barriers that lay between. But her omission would have to wait. Star had torn herself from Rachel's arms and was running like a little whirlwind to meet Cole. When Cole reached down to scoop her up, Rachel—dimly aware that the others were crossing safely—ran, too. And Cole, dripping from head to toe, reached out a free arm to embrace her as a man embraces his own family.

As if in a dream, Rachel helped set up the camp once all the wagons were on the far side. To her relief, there was a lot of merrymaking. And in the midst of it all, Brother Davey mounted Cole's stallion, allowed the animal to rear experimentally, and called out in a voice much like a raucous crow: "Prayer meetin' tonight fer all who's thankful fer a safe crossin'!"

22

"God Washed the Earth!"

The last "Amen" intoned, most of the campfires were extinguished—except for the few that twinkled here and there like lost fireflies. Tired families retired early, but Rachel lingered outside the wagon for a few minutes, hoping Cole would return soon. For some unaccountable reason, she felt uneasy. At last, deciding it was the mugginess of the night air, she crawled into the small tent where Aunt Em and Star were sleeping.

Unable to close her eyes, Rachel lay very still, going over the events of the day. Her heart soared with the memory of togetherness she had felt, first with Star and then with Cole holding the two of them. But the soaring did not last when she recalled the hateful scene with Julius Doogan. *What secret*, she wondered, *was he harboring?* True, Mrs. Grant had managed somehow to glean just enough information to make her a threat in regard to Father's shameless antics. And perhaps she suspected that Cole had bid for her hand. But there was something more, something which had caused Cole himself to flinch. So it had to be more than their marriage...

Her thoughts were cut short by the sound of footsteps outside. She strained her ears, but all was silent again. About to dismiss the sounds as her imagination, Rachel was all but jolted from the mattress by the loudest blast of thunder she had ever heard. A dog barked excitedly, and then the whole world blazed up as fiery-tongued lightning licked the sky again and again. Hoping not to disturb Aunt Em and Star, Rachel crept to the front of the tent. What she saw through the parted flaps made her heart stand still. A hurricane-force wind was shredding some of the more flimsy tents to pieces and people were running wildly in all directions.

Somewhere above the howl of the wind she heard men's voices screaming out a warning for the women and children to seek refuge in the wagons. And then she heard Cole.

"Rachel—Rachel—get them inside the wagon—*quickly!*"

Reacting rather than thinking, Rachel grabbed Star with one arm and reached out to awaken Aunt Em with the other. "The storm...quick...the wagon!" she gasped.

Aunt Em was on her feet and, wrapped in quilts, they were running with the wind to their backs toward the Conestoga.

"Now, darling, listen to Mother," she whispered to the child. "Daddy's wagon is safe and strong—like he is. Do you understand?"

"Strong," little Star repeated. "I will be safe."

Then Rachel and Aunt Em again braced themselves against the force of the wind and rushed out to warn those who were trying to remain in tents. Rain had begun to fall, first in enormous, scattered drops, and then in torrents. Almost immediately Rachel was soaked to the skin, and by the constant flash of lightning, she saw rivulets of water forming puddles. At first, she was able to step between them until they become one enormous pool. A flash flood!

Lifting her sodden nightgown above the water, she ran toward the ruin of tents—trying to scream above the continuous roar of deafening thunder. It was no use. She would have to locate the persons who had panicked one by one. Some of the tents, she realized were being swept away. But the people! Where *were* all of the people!

And then the sky was split in half by the greatest bolt of all. Rachel felt a heart-stopping jolt course through her body as she was knocked from her feet and the lightning completed its cycle to ground just beyond her. Impervious to pain, Rachel was unaware that she had been shocked by the strike. Her numbed mind could only respond to the focus directly ahead. Women, in their terror, had crawled beneath their mattresses and were hugging their children close as a means of protection. But the mattresses were a heavy, sodden mass, and one by one they were being blown away by the relentless cruelty of the wind. Help. She must help. *Now!*

Dragging them, carrying them, pleading with them—and praying all the while—by supernatural force Rachel was able to lead most of the hysterical women and children to the safety of their wagons. Then, disoriented, she turned toward where she believed her wagon to be. But water had risen to her knees and in the deeper places to her thighs. If this kept up, the wagon beds would float away. *Oh, I must get to Star...and where can Cole be?*

The lightning had stopped. The world lay in total darkness.

"Cole...*Cole*...COLE!" She screamed his name again and again, but the wind sucked the words from her mouth to be swallowed up by the throat of the rain.

Rachel ran to the right, then to the left, only to be pushed back by the mighty hands of the wind. Her hair streamed about her in a wild, wet tangle—choking her at times—and she felt shreds of her night garment cling to her drenched body. And then there was a mighty boom, mightier in Rachel's throbbing head than the boom of the actual thunder. The very earth beneath her bare feet shook and she felt the raging floodwater rise up to meet her as she fell. Rachel did not struggle. She was too tired. And nothing seemed to matter anymore...

At first, she seemed to be floating on the surface of the flood, her body weightless—her spirit suspended somewhere between heaven and earth. Then, she was sucked into its murky depths where there was no light, no air, no life! Rachel clawed at the nothingness—which suddenly became pleasant. There was a hum of low, pleasant voices and someone was brushing her forehead, her cheeks, and the hollow of her throat with gentle kisses. "Wake up—oh, my precious, brave darling—"

Rachel was unable to open her eyes. And she wasn't sure she wanted to. The dream might go away...letting her sink forever into the dark waters...without Cole...or Star...

"*Star!*" Her eyes flew open in terror. "Where—where is she—and where am I?"

While her heart was crying out for the child she had abandoned, Rachel's eyes were searching the wagon in which she lay for some sign familiar to her. "Easy—easy—" Cole was whispering above her. "You've had a terrible jolt through you—not to mention all you went through out there, my blessed angel. You and Aunt Em saved them all, Rachel. Do you hear? *All!* You're in my other wagon—"

Rachel tried to sit up only to be gently pushed back by Cole's forceful hands. "Not yet—but if you will promise to rest afterward, I have a surprise for you. Promise?"

"Star—" Rachel whispered weakly. "The other wagon—"

"Promise!" Cole's voice was a command.

Feeling that a hand had closed around her throat, Rachel could only nod. If they had lost little Star, nothing mattered.

Cole shifted his large frame ever so slightly. And there, sitting primly with thin, brown legs crossed to make her look like a wee pixie, sat Star.

"I knew you would get well," she said solemnly. "Daddy told me. God told him, after He washed the earth."

23

A Little Larnin' Won't Harm 'Em!

The endless night finally grayed into dawn. Rachel was unable to doze, even though every fiber of her being cried out for rest. The sounds outside were disturbing in a way that spelled rebellion instead of thankfulness.

Brother Davey and Cole, who had gone out to reassure the grumbling men, came back to report that the little stream they had crossed so effortlessly the day before had now overflowed its banks for a quarter of a mile on either side, making it too deep to pass. With all else so bleak, it seemed only fitting that Agnes Grant should stick her face through the back of the wagon without invitation.

"Look! The water went clean over my boots—biggest mess ever I saw—and ever'body callin' on me t' getcha—"

"Stop complainin', Aggie. Sometimes I think you was born with colic! Now, tell me their problem—*not* yours!" Aunt Em said with impatience.

"Some folk've no consideration. Wouldn't y'know thet young Miz O'Grady'd choose t'give birth and us in such a mess? Wimmen folks sent me fer you—you bein' a granny-woman—"

"Midwife!" Aunt Em said tartly, as she began getting together a bundle of clean rags and some kettles. "I'll be there. You find extry sheets 'n git some water, Aggie."

"Me—always *me* folks call on—" Mrs. Grant's grumbling voice died away as Aunt Em took a minute to consult a sheaf of papers on which she had made copious notes.

"Never know what to 'spect 'zactly," she said as if to herself and then she read aloud: " 'Pennyroyal tea t'sweat you, boneset tea to clear you out, whey poured off'n buttermilk fer cramps...stumpwater fer warts. Well, we won't be needin' that!" she said with a chuckle. "He'll be a wart later on."

The capable woman leaned down to kiss Star's sleeping face. And then she was gone. Rachel, sensing that she too would be needed desperately today, rose slowly, tested her legs, and began searching for a change of dry clothing.

Ready to step from the wagon, Rachel was stopped by the sudden appearance of Brother Davey. "Ain't much place fer the sole of yor feet. Makes me feel kinda sorry for the dove Noah sent from th' ark. But I see you're willin' t' chance it." *He looks a little like Noah must have looked,* Rachel thought with amusement. *Perplexed but patient.*

She smiled at him. "It sounds as if you could use some help."

He nodded. She told him then about Aunt Em's call. He nodded again.

"Some woman, my Emmy-gal," he said gruffly, his face flushing like a ripe tomato. "Cole wants I should tell you to take care, but I see 'twon't do no good—"

As he would have turned away, he bumped into Agnes Grant.

"I come t' report," she began in the kind of high-pitched voice that betrayed she had come for something entirely different. "Hey!" she exclaimed, her voice raised in fake surprise at seeing Star. "What have we here? I *thought* I saw a strange face, but I couldn't believe my eyes. Part Injun, I'd be judgin' and it ain't gonna set well with th' others—you sneakin' th' half-breed's gonna cause talk—"

Brother Davey scowled at her.

"Plain t' see who's gonna start it! And this here ain't no half-breed. It's my granddaughter ye'r talkin' 'bout. And now, Aggie, jest what's the nature of that report you come t' give?"

Abashed, Mrs. Grant began to back away, practically tripping over her feet in haste.

"I—why, just thet it's gonna rain like this fer a week maybe."

"It's rained longer," Brother Davey proclaimed knowingly. "Rained fer forty days and forty nights once. Ain't apt t' break that record!"

When the woman was gone, he turned to Rachel.

"Well, Star'll give her tongue a-plenty to wag 'bout. We'll end up havin' th' most talked-about wagon in th' bunch— her tellin' ever'body, 'That 'un was borned on th' wrong side o' th' blanket!'"

The preacher guffawed with a certain pleasure he found in the words. Rachel laughed with him. It was good to laugh again.

• • •

The rains did not let up. After three days of relentless downpour, the people were depressed as they struggled through the mire. It would be futile to attempt a fire, so food was mostly hardtack biscuits thoughtful women had baked in advance for such emergencies and jerky, meted out in careful ration.

One plentiful item was milk. The faithful cows ate their fill from the sodden meadows and, satisfied, gave rich milk in return. Brother Davey observed that they were more grateful than the travelers.

It was strange, Rachel thought as she looked back on the dark period later, that it was the milk—such a boon to the meager diet—that caused the trouble. Not the milk really, but its source—the cows. Those who had no cattle, or only a few, began to quarrel with those who had greater numbers, charging that it was the cattle which were holding everybody back.

"Can y' believe them what accepts th' bounty's the very ones causin' the trouble?" Aunt Em shook her head in disbelief.

Rachel thought about it. "No, Aunt Em, I can't," she answered. "It has been such a source of joy for us to share from Cole's herd. Oh, not that we wanted anything in return," she amended quickly. Then, biting her lip thoughtfully, she said, "I guess I just don't understand people."

"Ah, now, dearie, don't go bunchin' 'em together. Somethin' tells me you've not been around a heap?"

"That's true." Rachel refrained from saying that, besides her mother and Yolanda, there had been only an endless line of scoundrels brought to her doorsteps. Remembering, she shuddered. And then, almost immediately, the mood was gone. She had no right to entertain such thoughts. Why, on this trip she had come to know so many good, kind, loving, and understanding people they were as hard to count as stars in the Milky Way.

Aunt Em was watching her facial expressions and smiled when the sad look went away. "We're headin' fer a Promised Land 'a sorts. And jest be rememberin' that the Chosen Ones is gonna stick together. Right now," she sighed, "it's like th' Lord tilted th' earth and all the loose folks fell into this wagon train!"

Outside the wagon, talk was growing louder. There were charges and counter-charges, many of them darkly-colored with profanity. Rachel glanced nervously at Aunt Em, but the older woman simply said, "Star, have ever you seen a newborn baby?" When Star shook her head solemnly, Aunt Em took her by the hand. "Rachel, we're gonna duck under a quilt and visit Miz O'Grady."

Rachel sat for a few minutes thinking once Aunt Em and Star were wading toward the O'Grady wagon. Maybe there was another way of bringing the people together. It was true that Brother Davey's efforts to gather the entire group for a worship service failed. But supposing she and Aunt Em tried something different?

When Aunt Em and Star returned, Star's little face glowed with an inner light as she murmured, "Bambino." Rachel shared her plan with the older woman then. What would she say to telling Bible stories, like the Joseph's-coat story, to the restless children? And she, Rachel, would work with some of the children with their handwriting and ciphering. They could work in shifts. Of course, they would have to go from wagon to wagon, there being no dry place. But, oh, wouldn't it be wonderful? Rachel's face was beaming. And by the time she was finished, Aunt Em's was beaming, too. Why, they could start a regular revival!

"I can take along the Joseph's-coat dress to show—"

"No!" The exclamation from Star, who had been listening in her usual adult manner, burst out so abruptly that both women were startled. It was the first time she had expressed fear, but there was fear in the great tormented eyes now. "It is *my* Joseph's-coat dress—mine, *mine!*" She held it close.

Pity twisted Rachel's heart. The little dress was more than a garment. It was the only thing the child owned. And, in some strange way, it was visible proof that love existed.

Rachel understood. Even as she pulled the child close and whispered words of reassurance, her own eyes automatically went to the wedding ring on her left hand. How many, many times had she—like little Star—clung to the ring for reassurance! Once it had flashed fire. But now, in the darkness of the dismal downpour, the diamond and the burnished gold on which it was mounted, had lost their sheen.

Suddenly she was aware that the bad moment had passed. Star and Aunt Em were discussing the idea of Star drawing pictures for the stories. Rachel let go of the child and concentrated on the ring. Surely it would show a bit of brightness if she twisted it on her finger. Trying was a mistake. The turning of the ring only served to show Rachel that, in losing weight on this trying journey, the ring no longer fit. It was as if it belonged to someone else. She wondered numbly if Cole had given it to the other girl before her.

Star was busy with the pencils and slate Aunt Em had hauled from a box. Rachel was unaware that Aunt Em's eyes were on the wedding ring until she spoke. "They've no light 'a their own, ya know. But just you wait for a shaft of sunlight and it'll pick up the glow!"

Rachel flushed. *What I need is the sunlight of Cole's love*, her heart cried out. She turned stricken eyes to Aunt Em and there she saw understanding. "That ring'll pick up its shine, dearie. Cole's distracted now . . . but there'll come a time."

Rachel nodded, wishing that she could explain—and ask. She had no right to expect more of Cole and it astonished her to have such thoughts. *How can I expect more than I bargained for?* Yet, without him, she faced a lightless future.

"Not so!" It was as if a Voice had spoken to her from On High. "You have Star and you have work to do."

With the Voice came an inner calm. "Do we have another slate?" she inquired. Aunt Em wasn't sure. But there was always charcoal, some she'd saved "fer makin' hominy outta horse corn and filterin' out poison from a body's system." And more would be easy to come by once the rains stopped, the wise woman assured.

But it was the rains which gave opportunity for the teaching. So there was no time to be wasted. Quickly, the two women collected every scrap of paper they could find, daringly ripping a wooden slat from some of the crates as well.

"Ready?" Aunt Em asked.

And it was Star who answered. "Ready," she said, holding up a picture which was a perfect replica of her Joseph's-coat dress. "And here's the boy who weared it—yes?"

"Why, you're a real artist!" Rachel said with a thrill of pride. She wondered anew where the child had come from and how she had come to know so much.

• • •

The "larnin' sessions" (as some of the parents called them) went better than either Rachel or Aunt Em had expected. The women moved from wagon to wagon and, after the initial suspicion was overcome, most of the mothers were elated. The only problems encountered were those voiced angrily by a great majority of the men who opposed the teaching of the Bible.

"What kind of a God's gonna let it rain like this, robbin' us of ever' hope we got—all gonna be sick with lung fever—and you wimmen got the nerve t' come here 'bouts sayin' Somebody up there loves our young'uns?"

Brother Davey heard one such outburst and made matters

worse by saying, "Good Brother, it rains on the just and the unjust alike! The Good Book says—"

His words went forever unfinished. The man ran at him with a shovel and said, "Skedaddle to Hades out o' here!" Brother Davey skedaddled.

Aunt Em soothed his ruffled feelings, then gently suggested that he stick with the men's work and let her and Rachel handle the "little bitsy ones." With that she gave Rachel a sly wink. Then, turning back to her husband, the wise woman made a comment Rachel would never forget.

"Ya know, Davey love, others kin hate us, but we win. Unless we hate in return. Then the devil wins!"

Brother Davey straightened his thin shoulders, the blades pointing sharply from beneath the ragged plaid shirt. "Well, he ain't winnin' *this* wagon train—not with me aboard!"

The children were pathetically glad to have something to occupy their time. They responded well to the schooling—even those forbidden to hear the Bible stories. And there was a bonus Rachel had not expected. Little Star was taken to their hearts. So even the nonbelievers agreed that "A little larnin' won't harm 'em!"

24

Division

The rains subsided. Skies, however, remained sullen—
much like the mood of most of the travelers. The men were
milling about like the cattle, some saying that another storm
would ride in on the tail of the one just past and that they
should be moving to higher ground. Others contended that
the rivers were overflowing all about them and crossing
was impossible. Agnes Grant, of course, said that either way
all of them were sure to be drowned.

Rachel was guiding the uncertain hand of a twelve-year-
old boy who confided that "Not nobody'd learnt him

nothin' before" when she overheard snatches of an alarming conversation outside. She was sure that one of the men's voices was Cole's. The other was that of Julius Doogan. She strained her ears as she helped the boy loop an "O."

"The people distrust you, Lord," Julius said. "And after all, just because you're financing some of these people, you have no right to dictate. They're onto you—"

"Meaning?" Cole's voice was dangerously low.

Doogan's laugh was insulting. "Meaning that you intend they'll repay you double or be serfs to your land. It's no secret you're in this for yourself."

There was silence during which Rachel held her breath. She had no idea what the men were talking about, but something warned of impending danger. Her hand shook as she demonstrated the joining together of the letters which would spell Billy Joe Williams, the boy's name. What had happened outside?

"So—what I'm saying is—" Julius began uncertainly again, "is that you should bow out, disappear, vamoose!" His attempt at wit sounded worn, thin, and hollow—the kind used by shallow men.

"Why don't we let the people decide for themselves, Doogan?"

"They've already decided!" The reply came too quickly to be convincing.

"I will believe that when I hear it from the majority." Cole's voice was as cold as steel. "I think the ground has dried off enough for us to meet together tonight—"

Billy Joe tugged at Rachel's sleeve to show his work with pride. "That's fine," she said softly. "Now make the 'J' a little larger and try again." All the while, she was listening.

But strain her ears as she would, the men's words eluded her except for fragmentary phrases which made no sense.

"You plan telling...yes, your marriage enters...example of extracting money...indebtedness...expose cargo...like before?" Those were Julius Doogan's words. Cole's voice was low—too low for her to make out the words—but in it there was depth and authority. She heard him say her name but could distinguish no more.

Rachel felt as if an icy blizzard had blown in across the plains. She finished Billy Joe's lesson sooner than planned, left him some practice work, and hurried to share what she overheard with Aunt Em. The older woman nodded silently, having overheard a similar conversation between her husband and the wagon master.

"Only diff'rence bein' they're on our side—which is t' say, dearie, the side 'a th' Lord!"

"There's going to be a division, isn't there?"

"I'd say so—and good riddance."

Sheer black fright swept over Rachel. The safety in numbers she had clung to would be gone. She began to shake as fearful images flashed before her. Couldn't they see they needed one another? But other images crowded in to blot out the dangers.

"Aunt Em, if you know the answer, tell me. Did some other woman wear this ring before me?" Her heart pounded as she waited. "Julius Doogan was saying some cruel things. I could tell. . ."

"Julius Doogan's possessed of a devil! But, yes, another woman wore the ring, Rachel. And you'd oughta feel honored to be wearin' it now. 'Twas Cole's mother's weddin' ring."

For reasons only a woman can understand the two women burst into tears. When Rachel felt a little hand reach out to take hers in unspoken comfort, she gathered Star to her, crying all the harder, wondering if children (and men!) understood tears of joy.

"Oh, Star, I love you—you and Aunt Em—"

"And Daddy?" The words were no more than a whisper.

"And Daddy—oh, Star, *yes*, you and Daddy are my world."

The little fingers curled around Rachel's warmly. "Daddy, and me, and *God*. He makes for us a heaven—yes?"

"Outta the mouths of babes," Aunt Em said, blowing

her nose noisily. "And now, let's get ready t' support our men."

• • •

The meeting lasted until after midnight. Aunt Em suggested that she, Rachel, and Star invite Mandy Burnside, Liz Farnall, and Opal Sanders with her twins to come join them in their vigil. It had not occurred to Rachel that Elsa O'Grady would be able to come as it was so soon after the baby's birth. But, happy to be "out of confinement" and tense from the waiting, she shook the flaps of the wagon timidly. The women welcomed her, then they joined hands in silent prayer while little Star happily played "house" with the new baby, the twins, and Moreover.

The candles burned low. And still there was no word. At last, at the sound of voices, Rachel could wait no longer. Seeing that Star had fallen asleep, she left the group and stood in the darkness waiting for Cole. A little crescent of moon found its way between the curtain of dark clouds which continued shifting uneasily about in the sky. By its pale light she could make out the ghostly outline of the large group of men. They were only a short distance away, but their voices were a low rumble. Rachel hoped it was a good sign.

Then the parley was over. Small groups clustered with heads together. One man's voice rose above the others. "So Julius Doogan will now be captain of the fast movers! Good bein' ridda them pesky cows." There was a rousing round of applause which grew even louder when another speaker added that it was better yet having a new leader—one who knew how to move a wagon train forward for a change!

To the other side of her, Rachel heard rather than saw another group congregating. Her people, she realized, when Brother Davey's voice rang out. His announcement pierced the night in a near-gloat.

"We'll rename ourselves the 'Cow Column,' brethren—good name seein' as how we're headin' fer the land flowin' with milk 'n honey!" Other voices blended in, making words indistinguishable.

Cole approached suddenly from another direction. Rachel stretched out her arms to him in comfort which he accepted. After a few wordless moments, Rachel could no longer contain her questions.

"Cole, what's happening? We've been praying and the women are all waiting to hear . . ."

He cut her off with a shake of his head. "Their husbands will tell them soon," he replied softly. "Hey," he changed the subject, "you shouldn't be out here in the damp. I have to make some preparations for morning, so you go back inside now."

As her broad-shouldered husband turned her by the shoulders toward the wagon, Rachel swung around and clasped him around the neck, burrowing her head in his chest.

"Could you just . . . I mean, I want to tell you . . ."

"Yes?" Cole answered gently, expectantly. "Are you afraid?"

Her nerve lost, Rachel nodded yes. *I must tell him how much I care, how I've changed my mind about him, how I . . .*

"Yes . . ." she hesitated, "that's all I wanted to say." *I just can't tell him! What would he think?*

"Don't worry. Now inside with you!"

"I need a little more fresh air. Please, Cole."

"All right, but don't linger too long. Good night, my love." And he disappeared past the ring of flickering wagon lights again, leaving her questions unanswered and her need of him unsatisfied.

As she leaned against the wagon, Rachel pondered the strangeness of the human race. *How can anything so trivial as those with or without cows be the deciding factor as to whether a group—so much in need of one another on this*

perilous a journey—should divide themselves? There was
more behind it—the mumbling, the grumbling, and the
little innuendos purposely dropped. Cargo . . . previous trips
. . . indebtedness. Even Cole's marriage to me. What does it all
mean? And how many of the factors, if any, contributed to
this breaking apart of the wagon train?

Buried in thought, at first Rachel did not see the shadowy
outline that appeared from out of the darkness. *Had Cole*
returned? Did he sense her need for him after all?

And then there was a move so sudden Rachel was almost
swept from her feet as she was caught in a grip of iron,
a strong hand clamped over her mouth.

"Be still!" The warning was only a rough whisper, but
Rachel recognized the voice. *Julius!* In the secret heart of
hers there had always been fear of this man. Now a panic,
blacker than anything she had previously known, squeezed
her insides.

Clawing at his arms, twisting and arching her body, she
sought to get free. But his grip was like a vise—squeezing
the breath—the very *life*—from her.

Oh, Cole, where are you? her heart cried out.

Julius Doogan's breath was hot against her ear. "It's no
marriage you have—we all know the truth—come with
me!" The words were thick and senseless like those of a
drunken man.

Dear God, help me. With the prayer in her heart, Rachel
somehow managed to free her right hand and bring it
across the face of her accoster, sick with the feel of tearing
flesh.

With a howl of rage, he let her go. "Ask your lover what
he's hauling!" With that, he fled.

25

A Half-Beaten Enemy

After the division, things went better for the "Cow Column." The rains stopped. So did the murmuring. Aunt Em said time and time again what "an awful joy" it was to be rid of Agnes Grant. Rachel made no comment but felt that the woman's physical presence would have made little difference. She had already left behind a trail of doubt and misgivings, as had Julius Doogan.

But it was for reasons unknown to the others that Rachel found solace in Mr. Doogan's parting. Try as she would, Rachel was unable to erase the dreadful memory of his unwelcome caresses and his insulting manner. And time after time she wondered what he had meant by his parting taunt. That Cole could be hauling anything illegal was out of the question. So she tried to put the matter to rest.

Still, if only I could talk with Cole, find some answers to all the many questions. But he said to just trust him. That's just what I'll have to do!

In work, she found solace. And certainly there was plenty to do. She and Aunt Em decided that the lessons should go on. So, even after a hard day's driving, the two of them gathered the children around them.

"We'll have t' use the old scatter-gun approach," Aunt Em laughed. "Too many of 'em t' get in ones 'n twos like before."

That was true. And, oddly enough, the division had unexplainably sifted out the objectors of Bible teachings from the travelers. So Aunt Em's stories and little Star's pictures were in great demand, as were Brother Davey's services. At night, when the campfires burned low, he led the people into group prayer. Even those who had seemed so shy at first began to join in once they discovered that it was all right to "jest talk" to God instead of "usin' fancy words."

Cole, Buck, and Brother Davey were busier than ever. The caravan had divided in about half, the wagon master reported, but there was still just as much work to be done. The three men worked very hard, however, at holding the group together and keeping morale high. Somewhere along the widely-separated trails they finally lost sight of the "Cowless Column."

Rachel expressed a feeling of relief. Brother Davey said a loud, "Amen!" But Buck remarked, in his usual quiet manner, "I don't know that we should celebrate their going like that."

"Injuns?" Brother Davey asked, eyes betraying concern. Buck hesitated. "We do have unfriendly territory to cross;

but the route they chose is even more dangerous. I feel a grave concern—"

"Is there somethin' else troublin' ye then?"

Buckeye Jones glanced at Rachel, his dark eyes grave with concern. Somehow she felt that concern centered around her.

"It's just that a half-beaten enemy will seek revenge."

26

A Near Revelation

Rachel, who clung to Cole's every word as if it were a precious stone, was pleased when he said, "You have become more of a pioneer woman than I could have hoped for, Rachel."

He made the comment as he hitched the team for her. "Thanks to your driving this wagon, we're making ten miles a day now. We'll soon be crossing to the valley of the Platte River in the Nebraska Country. There's to be a celebration tonight. One of the men shot a buffalo. And," he lowered his voice in a whisper, which thrilled her clear through, "I thought that if we could slip away from our beloved shadows—namely, one child and one dog—maybe we could talk? Just you and I alone?"

The women were able to gather enough mesquite wood for a fire while the men dug a pit which children danced merrily around.

"Let them do the work for a while, darling Rachel—look at those lovely little hands all calloused." Cole took her hands, raised them to his lips, and kissed each rough, tender spot. "Now, if I could kiss away the ache in your heart—" Then Cole led her away to a quiet spot.

All of Rachel's loneliness and confusion welded together in one upsurge of yearning that would no longer be denied. Without her usual reserve, she blurted out, "All that's wrong with my heart is uncertainty, Cole. All I want, all I ever wanted was your love—"

Then, abashed at what she had dared to say, she stopped. Her breath came in little short gasps. And she felt the blood siphoned from her face in surprise that she had actually declared herself to a man who had not declared himself to her.

But why shouldn't she? She was his wife. Like Aunt Em said, if she had a question, she should come right out and ask it. Jutting her chin out just a bit, reminiscent of the old Rachel who had defied her father upon demanding a husband she could respect, Rachel raised her eyes.

When they met Cole's, she read a tenderness that surprised her. She heard his quick intake of breath.

"What is it, little Rachel? Tell me."

"The other girl, Cole—the one you took with you on one of the initial trips. What was she to you?"

To her surprise, Cole's gray-green eyes showed astonishment, then relief. "What have they been telling you?" The words were torn from him. "Haven't you suffered enough without senseless gossip? I can explain. I only wish all else was that simple . . ."

"Who was she, Cole? What happened?"

Tears choked her voice. And then Cole was gathering her into his arms, holding her snugly in the beautiful way a woman wants to be held by the man with whom she wants to spend the rest of her life.

Her pulse beating wildly in tempo to the music nobody else heard, Rachel listened. There had been another girl, yes, daughter of the family with whom his own family had been friends for generations. Love her? Yes, he had loved her as one loves a sister.

"Miriam's father was with my father in the import-export business. Both traveled extensively and we played together as children. It was expected we would marry and," he smiled, "somehow we never got around to telling them that we were not in love."

"But I don't understand—the trip—?" Rachel spoke from the spot near his heart where her head fit so well.

Cole's lips brushed her forehead gently. "I was transporting merchandise for Miriam's father to build a town. Unfortunately, some of it being guns for battling the British in case of attack caused accusations along the trail that I was supplying the British with weapons. Do you understand?"

Rachel nodded. "And Miriam?"

"The families on the wagon train became disoriented. There was friction, followed by division. And then the Indian raid which gave a hostile tribe the powerful weapons." When his voice died to a whisper, Rachel reached up her arms and drew his head to her chest.

"Oh, Cole—oh, my poor darling—what you have suffered. Aunt Em told me about your family—and now this—"

"I have suffered no more than you," Cole said and something in his eyes broke the lovely spell into which the conversation had led her. "If only you could share the dream of the town with me—"

"What is it, Cole—something more about Miriam?"

For a moment he hesitated. "My heart broke over what

happened to Miriam. She died of lung fever and in a sense I blamed myself. . .and certainly there were many others who blamed me for the trail I took. I grieved for her as one grieves for any dear friend. But, no, Rachel, it is not for Miriam that I am grieving now. I have asked you to trust me—and I ask that again, for what I am about to tell you—"

But the words went forever unfinished. There was the brassy sound of a bugle. Then everyone was shouting at once. "Come—and—get—it! Buffalo steak, coffee, biscuits. *Cole*, COLE!"

Cole looked at Rachel with eyes that were genuinely sorry. "We can't ignore them—"

Of course, they couldn't. Little Star, holding onto Moreover's ruff, was running like the wind to grab their hands.

"Come, come! A fiesta! Come, Mother. Come, Daddy."

The three of them joined hands and, laughing, tried to race Moreover back to the feast. All was in a wild jamboree of happiness.

"Hurrah for the Platte! We'll reach 'er tomorrow!"

The fiddling began, nobody realizing what lay between them and the Platte.

27

Vengeance is Mine, Saith the Lord

The unfinished conversation with Cole hung over Rachel as she guided the team with expertise on toward the Platte River. While she searched for some plausible explanation for his inability to love her fully, her heart sang with a certain joy at the same time. Even though there remained more to be said, Cole had told her enough to release her from wrestling with a shadow over which there could be no victory. For, as they talked the night before, she felt the ghost of a girl who was her imagined rival slip away.

And now Rachel dared dream that her marriage in name only to the man she loved could become a marriage in every beautiful sense of the word. She would share his dream of building a town. What a beautiful adventure for the two of them! It was obvious that Cole, while far from a rich man, possessed considerable means. And he was a businessman. He would know how to go about the matter. The sense of adventure, left to her by her frontier forefathers, rose up anew. And in place of the barren lands before her, Rachel saw a country store which would supply the needs of the settlers: bolts and bolts of bright calico; barrels of flour; and shovels, hoes, and plows for cultivating the rich, virgin soil; even a church with a spire.

Dreaming did not slow her pace. By this time fording streams was easier because Cole had shown the group how to organize and go about it. Easier, too, because there was no bickering.

Then, without the faintest warning, the world turned upside down. Cole, who was scouting ahead of the train, was signaling for the wagons to halt before Rachel had so much as seen the dust rise from the now hard-breathing stallion's feet.

"Down! Down into the wagons quickly—and *don't move!*" Cole's command was to the women and children. In the same breath he had ordered the men to arm themselves and circle the wagons.

"Get down flat, darling," Rachel whispered to little Star. The child, always unquestioningly obedient, flattened herself on the floor of Cole's "Wagon Number Two," which Rachel had driven since the division of the caravan.

Some part of Rachel's mind was marveling at the child. Another part marveled equally at the lack of panic in the other travelers. But over and above those layers of thought was the question: Indians? Bandits? And to her total surprise, Rachel felt no overwhelming fear. Instead, her trust lay completely in her husband—and in his trust in the Almighty.

I am Cole's wife and whatever he faces, I face with him. Her tie was as elemental as earth and fire. *Whatever happens we will cling to each other as only two loving people do who have too long endured a long separation.*

A lifetime seemed to flash before her. Actually, it was a matter of seconds from the time Cole sounded the alarm until he was inside the wagon with Rachel and Star.

"Highwaymen?" Rachel whispered as Cole reached for his musket.

In the gravity of the moment, there was no smile when he answered, "Bandits—looters—tuck the ring away quickly."

Rachel was pinning the wedding ring to a ruffle on her petticoat when Cole eased forward to look from the front of the wagon, only to draw back as the crack of a rifle split the air. The bullet splintered a rib supporting the canvas top, leaving an ugly tear where Cole's head had been.

"Cole!" The cry was wrenched from her and as she would have crawled to where he crouched, Cole waved her back.

Then in a low voice, he said, "I will need your help, Rachel. Move forward, so I can get to the opening in the floor."

Rachel obeyed. Cole, who had crawled around her toward the back, grabbed the very boards on which she had lain, and with a heavy tug, pulled upward. To her total amazement, there lay a cache of guns and what looked like an endless supply of gun powder—some of it made into bullets ready for use.

The wagon, she realized, *has a false bottom!* And then came the bitter memory of Julius Doogan's taunting question tossed at her during their unpleasant encounter the night of the division.

There was no way of knowing how long or how well Cole stalled off the would-be attackers. She knew only that there was a barrage of gunfire as her body hovered protectively over little Star's. The child, she noticed, had not moved. Her enormous brown eyes were open wide, the pupils enlarged, but in them she saw no fear.

"Daddy will take care of us—yes?" they seemed to say.

Through it all, Cole seemed calm. Loading, aiming, firing. And all the while, there were little inaudible words of reassurance for her and Star. Only once did Rachel lift her head to cast a glance through the widening gap of the canvas top which had now spread to the side. Through it, she caught a glimpse of masked men and found herself hoping, praying that (enemies though they were) there was no blood shed. And oh, how she prayed for Cole!

And then there was silence. When she was about to ask with great relief if the attack was over Cole put a warning finger to his lips. "They've gone for the horses. I must leave you—and I ask you to be brave. You will be needed if there are injuries among our people."

"Cole, no—" The words were torn from her. But he was gone.

At last it was over. Cole was back, lifting the boards and replacing the guns, then carefully closing the false bottom. His gray-green eyes, so translucent when they looked at her, were begging her to understand. *Understand what? That there must be violence? Or* . . . and her heart died a little within her then . . . *that it was true that he was transporting ammunition. Surely not to the Indians!*

She shook her head to clear it. As a loyal wife, Rachel must not think such thoughts. They were unworthy, belonging only to such scoundrel turncoats as Julius Doogan.

Star was scrambling up. Patiently, she waited—small face upturned—to be noticed by Cole. He reached down and gently scooped her up and wordlessly reached a free arm for Rachel. Just as wordlessly, she walked to him—letting her head rest against the reassuring rhythm of his heart.

"I was proud of my girls," he whispered huskily. "And now, Star, I ask that you stay here. Daddy will go for some of your friends to play with you. I have some little trinkets I had planned for Indian children in a box in the corner," he said pointing. "But you may take them out. Just don't leave the wagon."

"I will stay." Star's eyes sparkled with anticipation.

Outside the wagon, Cole paused. "Rachel, I must apologize. I hope you do not find me cruel . . . and that nothing I did aroused suspicion. There's more to say, but we must get to the others. Some are hurt—"

"Badly?" Rachel was surprised at the calm of her voice.

"I don't know, darling—and I am unable to check. I must look after the stock—prevent a stampede. They took some horses . . . and, Rachel, they slaughtered a number of our cows. I didn't want Star to see."

A little cry rose to Rachel's throat. "Oh, Cole, who—*why*?"

Cole bit his lip for control. "I don't know who." He lowered his voice as he pointed to Aunt Em who was running as fast as her ample body would allow. "I can only suspect."

The "Cowless Column." Cole might as well have said it. Rachel felt a great nausea that began in her stomach sweep over her and localize in her heart. Then, pulling herself together, she faced Emmaline Galloway, the woman whose strength of spirit had pulled her through so much already.

Hours later, as the sun was lowering, the wounded had been cared for. Women were going about the business of laying a fire for roasting the slain cattle. And men were assessing their losses. All, it seemed, had been robbed of their guns. There had been few to begin with except Cole's. But God had mercifully spared the lives of their people. Nothing else mattered. And so in the midst of what the less sturdy would have called disaster, someone began to hum, "The Battle Hymn of the Republic" and the others took up the refrain of "Glory, glory hallelujah!" There could be no doubt that God was marching on. And they marched with Him!

• • •

Some time later it was Star who pointed to the not-too-distant hill at the peak of their thanksgiving. And there, in what appeared to be an endless line, stood the stolen horses—and astride them, the Indians. Statue-still, guns mounted to their shoulders...and human scalps hanging from their belts!

The sight was far too horrible for Rachel to believe. Paralyzed, she stood seeing but not believing. The swell of pain was beyond tears.

*Dead? The ones who had left them were dead? Why, **why**, WHY? Because they had taken a more dangerous route...owned the horses...or was it the guns? Dead.* Hysteria rose to her throat, blotting out reality.

Then two familiar, strong hands were gripping her arms. *"Sing! Sing, Rachel—it's our only hope!"*

Sing, Cole, sing? How could she sing in this raw and primitive grief so new to her? When her mouth felt like old paper—dry and dusty? But sing she must. She took deep breaths until she was strong enough to raise her head, open her mouth, and let the words—which surely the Holy Spirit had given her—came.

> In the beauty of the lilies,
> Christ was born across the sea,
> With a glory in his bosom
> That transfigures you and me;
> As he died to make men holy,
> Let us *live* to make men free,
> Our God is marching on!

One by one, other voices—shaken, uncertain, and as anguish-filled as her own had been—rose, reaching a new glory.

And then the miracle happened. One of the men, his garishly-painted face and his feathered headdress setting himself apart from the braves at his side, raised a hand to those lined up beside him. At the signal, they turned and rode away.

Rachel never knew afterward who fell on bended knee first. Or maybe they all dropped at once. But the prayers that went up were long and fervent.

Rachel, totally unaware of the part she had played to help save them, came back to reality by the touch of a little hand.

"We are safe, Mother mine. God droved them away with Daddy's help—yes?"

Gathering the deceptively fragile body to her, Rachel held her tight, comforting herself as well as the child. And all the while she was listening to announcements the men were making. The Indians, should they return, would not come back during the night hours. Tomorrow there must be no fires. And departure must be long before daybreak. All nodded in accord. And then came the question all had dreaded.

"Is it—was it?" Liz Farnall's voice broke and her husband finished for her.

"The scalps—could they have been from the group who pulled away from us? I recognized my horse—" His voice, too, broke.

Cole's voice when he answered was firm, yet gentle. "There should be no secrets between us—no false hopes. So, yes, I must tell you that there can be no doubt. Now, as to how many were killed, there is no telling." He said a few more words, but Rachel was past hearing. They would help if they found survivors, she believed he said. . .but the rest was lost on the night air.

Dear Lord, her heart cried out, *forgive them for they know not what they do.* And Rachel herself could not have told another whether she was speaking for the savages or the people they had slaughtered—or both.

Quietly, fires were extinguished. Guards were posted. Every precaution was taken. And still the people stood huddled, as if finding solace in their fellow travelers.

Brother Davey muttered, " 'Vengeance is mine,' saith the Lord."

There were a few faint "Amens." And then Buckeye Jones, the trusted wagon master everyone depended on, stood up and said in his usual shy voice, "If I might share with you the words of St. Francis?" His offer was unexpected and turned all faces toward him in surprise. His voice, though quiet, was a deep baritone with a consoling quality:

Lord,
Grant that I may not so much
Seek to be consoled as to console;
To be understood as to understand;
To be loved as to love;
For it is in giving that we receive;
It is in pardoning that we are pardoned.
And it is in dying that we are
Born to eternal life.

Silence fell over the group. Rachel could feel their tears in the darkness. Then, quietly—as Arabs fold their tents—they folded the troubles of the day. Tomorrow was a new day—a day that would bring them to the Platte.

Families, drawn together more closely in view of the new tragedy, clung closely to each other as they turned toward their tents.

28

Message at Ft. Laramie!

They traveled hard the next day over rough country. Rachel, still bearing the heavy burden of the night before, did not ask for a relief driver so she could walk. Nothing mattered now except reaching the Platte. She allowed little Star to skip alongside her wagon, her thin brown legs racing beside her furry shadow, Moreover, but never letting the two of them out of her sight. The train did not even stop for a noon meal.

Then, just as the sun was sinking below the bleak sand hills, the scouts caught their first view of the wide and beautiful valley below. Cole rode back to tell Rachel that they must eat a cold supper. There was no fuel and no matches. It was possible to fire a musket into a heap of dead leaves to start a fire, but too risky. They must not take safety for granted. The Indians could be trailing them. Rachel was too exhausted to care—other than for their safety. Time and place had lost their meaning once again.

Day after day they pushed westward up the south bank of the Platte, sometimes in storm, sometimes in burning heat. There were only buffalo paths to follow now down to the river. The paths were deep and jagged so following or crossing them was jarring some of the wagons to pieces.

Cole's wagons were sturdier. More so, Rachel realized, because of their double bottoms. And with such thoughts came the memory of what she was hauling. Try as she would to put all doubt behind her, the idea was more bothersome than she dared admit even to herself. After what she had seen, the possibility of anyone's putting deadly weapons into the hands of hostile Indians was more than her tired mind could cope with. *Surely,* she told herself, *it must be the strain and the unbearable heat that allows me to indulge in such thinking.*

Past the point where the North and South Platte came together, the trail-weary group had traveled eighty-five miles up the south branch before the men decided they should try to cross. When Cole told Rachel, she sensed anxiety in his voice—an anxiety she put into words.

"The river's high, Cole. Dare we try?"

He hugged her to him—their first embrace in a long while. And the feel of his warm body next to hers removed all fears, all suspicions, all doubts. Had any woman ever loved as she loved? Finally, Cole spoke the words she had waited so long to hear.

"I love you, darling Rachel—I love you, *love* you!"

Joy bubbled up inside her. Making her want to laugh, to cry, to praise God. So wrapped was she in a silken cocoon of euphoria that she hardly took notice of Cole's leaving.

He loves me! He loves me! Over and over her heart played the ageless tune of all women in love. It sang on as the men built boats by stretching two buffalo hides around each wagon box and letting the hides dry. The hides were then rubbed with tallow as women made lunches and hot coffee for the workers to keep up their morale. Rachel's heart continued its song in sweet refrain as the first boat—manned by six men with Cole and Buck on either side—started across the river. They would make it. Of course, they would. The tallow-rub had made the wagon-bed boats airtight. And Cole, as much in love as she, could lick the world single-handedly. And then there was the protection of the other men who swam alongside, pulling ropes.

Other women stood on the bank of the river and wrung their hands when one of the men yelled, "Move left—hurry, *hurry*—we've hit quicksand!"

But Rachel, whose heart vibrated with the new strength of her husband's declaration of love, stood quietly. The men would make it to the other side. They had to. Before her lay a whole new life with Cole. Then others, seeing the composure of her face, took strength. And an air of calm prevailed.

Nevertheless, there was no denying that she felt a powerful relief when it was all over. As the others gathered around her to thank her for her strong faith, Rachel could only quote what she recalled Aunt Em's having said at the beginning of the trip: "God gives us all the faith we need. We only have to be sure we have faith in the right things!"

The words surprised Rachel herself. She felt a great surge of elation at her newly-found objectivity—her ability to cope, to trust, to believe.

I started this journey a girl and on it I became a woman, she marveled to herself as the others moved away.

Aunt Em moved closer to her and remarked, "Seems

to me you're wearin' a mighty satisfied look these days. Like you'd been in the cookie jar—but not caught at it!"

Rachel, her eye on Cole who was swimming back for his own wagon, his wife, and daughter, felt herself color. Aunt Em gave her a knowing look. "Pretty wonderful, ain't he?"

Once across the South Platte and following up the north branch, travel was much more rapid. Buck passed the word that the train was moving at the unheralded clip of sixteen miles a day! That brought a rousing cheer from the tired travelers and morale shot even higher as they passed the landmarks they had read about in letters from friends and family who had passed this way before: Cedar Grove, Solitary Tower, the Chimney, and Scott's Bluff. Rachel, too, was happy and relieved. This meant that Cole and Buck deemed it safe to work their way back to the more familiar passage of the Applegate Trail now—some of the danger being past.

• • •

In mid-July the wagon train neared Ft. Laramie. On the evening before, Cole made the announcement that they would be arriving about noon but advised against the purchase of more supplies than was essential.

"Their prices are unreasonable," he said. "Bear in mind that we're on the main trail now and there are always people who make profiteering from the helplessness of others a way of life."

Something about Cole's warning took Rachel back to the past that she had all but forgotten on this trip. Cole might well have been describing her unprincipled father, the man who would have auctioned off his own flesh and blood! How far away from that world the journey had brought her— or was it just the distance? No, it was more the love and respect she felt for her husband, her joy in little Star, the gentle understanding of friends they had gathered around them, and a deeper, more abiding faith in the omnipresence of God. The past was over—done with. Ahead lay a life that was more than she and Yolanda, in their wildest girlhood dreams, could have imagined.

Thinking of her friend reminded Rachel to ask if there would be a way she could mail a letter at Ft. Laramie.

"Thanks for reminding me, Rachel," Cole said more to the group than to her. "There will be. Also, there's a chance some of you may have mail there—"

The rest of his words were drowned out by cheers. Rachel busied herself thinking of the quick letter she would send ahead to let Yolanda know she would be coming—with a husband and daughter! She went to sleep with a smile on her lips in anticipation of Yolanda's surprise.

The stopover in Ft. Laramie was brief. Prices were as high as Cole had warned. The people were unfriendly and, as Brother Davey remarked, obviously out to "skin folks alive."

Rachel overheard a bearded man, wearing a sleeveless jerkin without a shirt underneath, say, "Flour's a dollar a pint. Take it er leave it!"

The customer left it.

Rachel felt uneasy and anxious to be underway again. But there was more delay since several of the wagon tongues had to be replaced. Cole came to tell her and suggested that she might wish to spend some of the time tutoring the children and shouldn't she get a bit of rest? Rachel was nodding, her heart in her eyes.

"Don't look at me like that, little bunny-face," Cole teased. "Your husband's got work to do." Together they laughed and then he suggested that she could help by checking on the mail when she posted her own letter.

The proprietor was discourteous, having discovered that here was a wagon train which was no easy market for his overpriced merchandise. He fumbled with the stack of mail much longer than was necessary, asking Rachel time and time again to spell her name. At last, he shoved a bundle of letters plainly marked "Lord" at her. She was about to thank him when her eye came to rest on an envelope on the very top which was addressed to her.

Surely there must be some mistake. Cole would have left word for his business mail to be sent through by means of relay ponies which brought the mail from St. Joseph. *But who would be writing to me?* she wondered as she ripped open the envelope addressed in the spidery handwriting with an obviously expensive quill.

The business address at the top was that of an attorney and the inside address read: MRS. RACHEL BUCHANAN LORD. So there could be no mistake. Oh, but there was! There *had* to be! Her head was spinning—or was the dingy room crowded with weary travelers whirling? Everything had gone out of focus with the letter's first words. Try as she would, Rachel could not make out the words—the awful words—that some unknown attorney had written. She grabbed for support. And, failing to find it, crumpled in a helpless little heap on the hard dirt floor.

29

Ending a Marriage

Consciousness had returned, but Rachel was unable to open her eyes. She had the vague impression that someone was cradling her in tight, protective arms, and whispering words of endearment. The voice was like an echo from an empty tomb. And, mercifully, for the time being, she could remember nothing. Cole must be holding her, but . . .

When memory came it was so sudden that Rachel sprang from the arms which held her like a captured animal. And her voice was clear, in spite of the pain which twisted her heart dry.

"The letter," she said with no inflection, "is it true?"

"It is true that you are the sole owner of your childhood home—that the mortgage has been met—"

"On what terms?" Rachel felt her fists bunch at her sides as she waited for the words which would change her life one way or the other forever.

"Rachel!" The word was torn hoarsely from his throat. "Listen to me—I've tried so many times to explain. And I've prayed the nights away trying to find a way to tell you—"

"On what terms?" Rachel repeated with no more inflection than before.

Cole took a quivering breath. "I met your father's terms, Rachel—gave him enough to live on, and gave him the right to live in the house unless you deem otherwise—"

"In exchange for a wife! No, a *woman*—you didn't want a wife." The tear-smothered words were barely audible. "And you let me ask *you* to bring me. Oh, can't you see what you've done to me? I could die of shame."

"Don't, Rachel—please don't, my darling. It is I who feels ashamed that I haven't somehow found the courage to tell you. I was a coward and afraid of losing you. But, as to not wanting a wife—oh, my darling, if only you knew how I've fought to control the love you stir in me—how I've prayed—"

Rachel would have expected anger to rise up as an ally, or a loathing so strong that it would put the man who had betrayed her out of her heart forever. But she felt neither. Instead, there was only emptiness.

Cole was pleading with her again. "It was the only way, Rachel. If only you will try to remember how your father threatened us...vowed to humiliate you. Oh, I'm not defending what I did. It was wrong to deceive you. Just know that marriage was my idea. And only God Himself knows how much I love you—have loved you from the start—"

"Love?" Rachel her own voice, stifled and unnatural. "I

don't understand your definition. There has to be trust—you told me so yourself."

"So I did, my darling. But you said you could never marry a man you could not respect—and that included all those unwelcome suitors—"

Rachel rose on an elbow, her face blanched of color, she knew, because there was no blood left in her body. "And it includes you, Cole."

"Rachel—" Her name was torn from him.

"Please go," she said tonelessly. "You have done your part and more, Cole. You have bought and paid for me. You have brought me West. I have no complaints. And," Rachel tried to control the quiver in her voice, "I will keep my promise. I will release you when we reach Oregon."

"And supposing I don't wish to be released?"

Summoning her last reserve of strength, Rachel said, "You can't hold me against my wishes. Please go."

Cole caught hold of her shoulders, forcing her to look into his face. How haggard he looked! But she would not let herself fall under his spell again. Never. *Never!*

"Look at me, Rachel. Tell me that you don't love me. Make me believe it—and I will go!"

When she did not speak, he released her. "I had no right to ask that." Then he was gone, ending a marriage that never began.

30

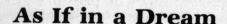

As If in a Dream

For several days the way led up the Platte. Rachel performed her duties as if in a dream. She watched unemotionally as one part of the company crossed over by lashing canoes together and tying watertight barrels at the side for "bobbers." Then the wagons were placed aboard.

There were some whoops of joy when they bade the Platte good-bye and turned westward up its branch, the Sweetwater, toward Independence Rock. But Rachel did not take part in the festivities. When camp was pitched at the Rock, many carved their names on its molten sides. Rachel, however, took little Star for a walk, feeling alive only in the presence of the small being she still felt God had purposely sent into her life.

When they returned to camp, Star begged to look at the words that had been carved in the Rock. She was fascinated with the scratched lettering. And then she let out a squeal of delight. "It's a heart, Mother mine. Look!"

Rachel looked, then she, too, let out a little gasp.

"What says it, Mother? Tell me!"

Trying hard to keep her voice steady, Rachel read: "Cole, Rachel, and Star Lord."

Star began to dance and clap, showing more emotion than Rachel had ever seen from the child. "Our names—*ours*! And in a heartful of love—yes?"

With tears streaming down her face, Rachel was compelled to say truthfully, "Yes, darling, a heartful of love." For it was clear to her now that no matter what Cole had done, she was in love with her husband. And, being a one-man woman, she always would be.

• • •

After several days at Independence Rock, the party moved on. Rachel understood that there would be no more buffalo beyond the continental divide and that the men would try to make a good hunt here. That made sense since supplies were low.

As they drove on, word passed along the line that hunters had brought in some fine antelope and two fat young buffalo. That meant a feast. The night delivered a blue vault of sky, bright with stars. And on the ground, the brightness of the campfires rivaled the lamps of heaven. Someone fiddled. Set after set danced after the feast.

To Rachel's surprise, Brother Davey danced out in the middle of the group and called loudly for Aunt Em to join him. Rachel was smiling at the happiness she read in Aunt Em's face—happiness born of the shared moment with her husband. There had been so few, she thought to herself, then Star was tugging at her arm.

"Dance!" she cried, her velvet eyes wide with excitement. "Daddy wants to dance with us!"

She had not seen Cole come toward them. And now she hesitated, torn by a conflict of emotions she had given up trying to understand.

Then, as if drawn by some magnet, she was on her feet and the three of them were whirling madly about the campfire. Cole returned Rachel and Star to where they had been sitting.

Surely he will say something. And if he does? Rachel found herself wanting to hurt him and make him love her at the same time—which made absolutely no sense. But suddenly she didn't want to hurt him at all. . .

But neither does he want me, she supposed. With a faint smile, he walked away, leaving her with the bright-eyed child who asked her how fire came to be. Rachel told her several of the Indian legends she knew, her mind on Cole to the point that she hardly realized little Star's head was drooping until the long, dark hair fell in a screen about her face, and with a little sigh of satisfaction, she snuggled against Rachel's breast.

31

Down the Western Slope

The crossing of the mountains at South Pass had seemed so easy that it hardly seemed like a crossing at all. The entire caravan had been excited over the view of the eternal snows of the Rocky Mountains and the pass was wide and flat.

Now the slope ran westward, the streams all running toward the Pacific. Cole and Buck engaged an aged fellow who called himself "Mountaineer Joe" to guide the train along the Green River to the Bear River. The mountainman operated a little trading post and from him the men were able to replenish the ebbing supplies.

There was a tense moment when the party encountered a large number of Indians. But Mountaineer Joe waved and greeted them in English. To the astonishment of all, one young buck scratched his head and, looking at the long train in wonder, said, "Are there any palefaces left where you come from?"

Cole, with Star's help, passed some of the little trinkets to the Indian children. Then, as the tired travelers stretched their legs, Cole asked the young Indian man to take him to his chief. When an older Indian rode up in full headdress, Cole motioned for him to follow. The chief dismounted and the two of them walked to the back of Cole's "Wagon Number Two" which Rachel had been driving. The wagon with the guns!

Oh, dear God, no! her heart cried out. *Not this. Whatever else he has done, real or of my dark imagining, don't let him trade guns to the Indians. . .*

Her prayer was cut short when Star darted out of reach to follow Cole. "No, Star, *no*—come back—"

But, like a tiny butterfly, Star—with Moreover at her heels—was out of earshot. Rachel, her legs trembling until they would hardly support her, ran in a vain effort to catch her.

By the time Rachel reached the wagon, Cole had rolled up the side of the canvas and crawled inside, leaving the entire view exposed to what a child should not see. Transfixed in horror, she watched as Cole ripped up the boards as he had done before. Then, cleverly managing to push the cache of guns beneath a side seat, he dug deeper.

Rachel gasped. *A third floor? What did it mean?* And then she saw him rise from his feet, holding what appeared to be a book in his hand. Hundreds of others lay on the previously hidden floor.

Star was watching in fascination. As was the Indian. "Book that speaks—like man in black robe say?" he asked in awe.

"Yes," Rachel's numbed ears heard Cole say. "It speaks of God's love for all the peoples of the earth and how they can live in peace through believing in Him."

"I believe, Daddy," said little Star. *Oh, the miracle of the child!* Rachel's heart was filled with the love of God that passes all understanding.

But what was this? The old Indian was climbing back on his horse. And with something that resembled a toothless grin, he said to Star. "Believe!" Then he rode away with his Bible.

Rachel wanted to rush to Cole, to throw her arms around him, to apologize. But he was busy rolling down the sides of the canvas and Aunt Em was calling her. The time was not yet right.

● ● ●

Rachel marked September 1st in her almanac. This was the day, Buck had revealed the night before, when they would be approaching the Portneuf River Valley. A time to be glad of heart. And yet there was a spell of gloom cast on the travelers because Cole had told them openly that this was where he had to turn another direction on his second attempt to lead a train through to Oregon.

Were they willing to try? Yes, they all agreed.

Aware of the dangers, they headed toward the sagebrush plains of Idaho. Trails, they found, spread out in all directions. And for the first time the company became, if not disorganized, at least separated. Friends and families clung together. The loners made their way as best they could— alone or in small groups.

Rachel forced herself to push ahead, following directions, not thinking. She hardly noticed, so numbed from the journey was she, as they crossed the right bank of the Snake River, doubled back to the left bank at Fort Boise, and drove their teams up the narrow log-strewn valley of Burnt River, down into the valley of the Powder River. Another divide waited to be crossed into the valley of the Grande Ronde.

Cole rode back to speak with her. "This is almost the end, Rachel, and no words can express my admiration for your courage. You have furnished strength for the other women. But," he hesitated and then lowered his voice so that, hopefully, little Star would not hear, "there's a bad stretch ahead—the Blue Mountains. There'll be a guide, but can you handle it?"

Rachel nodded that she could.

Her confidence was uttered before realizing that huge trees barred the trail. But there was the reassuring sound of axes ringing through the forest. They would make it. *Act, push on, don't think . . .* and, using all the skill she possessed while breathing an unending prayer, she moved on out, aware only of little Star beside her. And Cole leading the way . . . as up, up, up they climbed.

Suddenly there was the deafening screams and cheers of what sounded like a thousand male voices. "The crest! We're at the top! The crest!"

The crest . . . the crest . . . the crest . . . a million echoes wound through the thick green of the forest.

But there was no time to stop for celebration. It was time for the first snows of winter to begin at this high altitude. So the wagons rumbled down the slopes at a dangerous speed, just ahead of the first snowfall.

There was time for nothing but travel—no talk, no long evenings about a campfire. The group hardly stopped at all except for brief rest periods during the darkest part of the night. Meals were sparse: cold biscuits, uncooked dried fruits, and a plentiful supply of the buffalo meat which the men had made into jerky.

And then they were at the point where the Walla Walla flows into the Columbia River. All manner of boats, rafts, and crafts were assembled—some carrying their earthly goods on the makeshift boats. But there was solace to be found in the fact that they were all reunited now.

Somehow they would make it, they said—and they did. For out of nowhere there appeared a man who introduced himself as Squire O'Rourke. The squire owned boats and—while he openly admitted that he would just as soon too many settlers didn't come to spoil his territory—he was a man of mercy.

"Not one to see me fellowman drown—not me!" So he loaded them onto his great boats and ferried them across.

Rachel was too exhausted to care whether she drowned on the way over—except that little Star would need her. And, of course, there were the Bibles. And Cole . . .

32

Journey's End

Oregon! They were here!

It was Star who, with the wisdom of a child, pointed at the beautiful valley that lay below them once they were in the new country.

"It looks like a Joseph's coat!"

Rachel, who was standing alone with her, feasting her own eyes on fertile fields, walled in by the surrounding hills wrapped in their eternal green robes, their peaks tasseled with snow, could only gasp with pleasure.

Here and there, mingling with the evergreens, were

deciduous trees kissed by the colors of autumn. And amid all this there were occasional log cabins, their yards still abloom with the last flowers of the season, and welcoming wisps of smoke rising from the fat stone chimneys.

Along the fence rows were wild apple trees, laden with fruit—and surely the greenery entwining the trees must be grapevines! Rachel swallowed hard, trying to imagine what a cold glass of the fruit juice would taste like to her parched tongue.

A place of mellow beauty—Joseph's coat indeed!

"Surely this must look like the Promised Land Moses was allowed to glimpse," she marveled.

"I know about Moses, Mother mine," Star answered, her eyes large and dark. She pointed to the largest and most magnificent of the snowcaps, saying, "Aunt Em told us about him. Maybe it's from that mountain that he brought the commands—yes?"

"Commandments," Rachel corrected gently. She was about to ask if Aunt Em ever told stories from the New Testament, when Rachel sensed that the two of them were not alone.

"It is almost too beautiful to be spoiled by words."

Cole! I would know the low, gentle voice if asked to pick it from a million others! Not trusting herself to speak, Rachel could only nod in agreement.

There was silence as the three of them watched a fat chipmunk come from the friendly shadows in search of one last nut for his winter supply. Star moved slowly toward the little animal, which had not moved but only given a flirt of his fluffy tail and continued to stare with beady little eyes. Star picked up a pine nut, offered it, and to the surprise of the two adults, the chipmunk came forward to take it from her hand. Rachel felt unaccountable tears fill her eyes.

"So," Cole inhaled deeply, "you will forgive me for intruding. But I believe I have something that belongs to you."

Rachel turned to him then and, seeing the tired sadness that passed over his face, felt her heart wrench inside her. And the tears, which had sprung to her eyes as she watched Star make her offering to the furry little animal, spilled over without warning. She turned away to hide them.

But Cole had already seen. "Why are you crying, Rachel?"

How can I answer? Her sense of loss was too great for words. When she lifted her eyes, the lashes still heavy with tears, the pain she felt still flickered there.

"The journey has ended," she said.

"We've come a long way together," Cole began and then he stopped. Without warning, his arms were around her. "Oh, Rachel, why are we talking like this? Can't we leave the shadows behind—begin anew—there's another journey ahead, the one that life has to offer—"

When his voice faltered and stopped, Rachel reached up to pull his head down for the first long kiss they had ever shared. When at last he lifted his head, both of them were shaken. And in his eyes was a look of such intense, deep love that seemed to wash over Rachel in a refreshing and cleansing wave.

"I told you I had something for you," he said softly. And with that he pulled his mother's wedding ring from his vest pocket. "It came loose from your—uh—"

"Petticoat," she laughed.

He colored and nodded. "And I found it among the Bibles in the wagon. Oh, Rachel, will you wear it—be my wife, my *real* wife—forever and ever?" The words were a whisper.

Rachel, whose heart was beating such a wild tattoo she was unable to speak, lifted a trembling hand to accept the beautiful symbol of commitment. She looked down at the ring and it was shining as it had shone the first night he placed it on her finger. The first, bright light of love was back—defying words. Their love, like the sparkle of the ring, would remain always ready to offer flashes of brilliance of a deeper, more abiding love than which she had once glimpsed.

They were still clinging together when little Star skipped back to wedge herself between them, certain of her welcome. Looking up into their faces with her great, dark eyes aglow, she smiled.

" 'Love one another as I have loved you.' The words of Jesus—yes?"

"Yes, little Star, the words of Jesus," Cole answered. As he gazed down at his wife and daughter, he added, "And with the grace of Jesus, we will continue together on this journey to love."